Bartolo Longo

History of the Sanctuary of Pompei

dedicated to the Most Blessed Virgin of the Rosary. Vol. 1

Bartolo Longo

History of the Sanctuary of Pompei
dedicated to the Most Blessed Virgin of the Rosary. Vol. 1

ISBN/EAN: 9783337299729

Printed in Europe, USA, Canada, Australia, Japan

Cover: Foto ©Andreas Hilbeck / pixelio.de

More available books at **www.hansebooks.com**

HISTORY

OF

THE SANCTUARY OF POMPEI

DEDICATED

TO THE MOST BLESSED VIRGIN OF THE ROSARY

BY

BARTOLO LONGO ESQ.

—

VOLUME I.

—

VALLE DI POMPEI

EDITING SCHOOL OF TYPOGRAPHY OF BARTOLO LONGO

—

1895

THE PRECEEDING EDITIONS

OF

THE HISTORY OF THE SANCTUARY OF POMPEI

The first time that a book, treating of the Sanctuary of Pompei, appeared, was in the month of January of the year 1879.

It was written by us, and edited in Naples, at our expense, by the Firm of Andrea and Salvatore Festa, in a little volume of 100 pages in-8.

We tried with all our might to make known to the good Neapolitans, (as we could not then dream that our undertaking would be received with so much enthusiasm, not only throughout Italy, but in many parts of the world besides) that a temple, dedicated to the Virgin Mary of the Holy Rosary was to be raised in Pompei, and that even before beginning the construction of the Sanctuary, the blessed Virgin had already worked several miracles. For which reason, having then no other desire in our heart than that of increasing the devotion of others towards her by the recital of such prodigious

events, which were the immediate cause of the
rapid progress of the new Temple, we did not
then entitle that little rolume, as should have
been done, « THE HISTORY OF THE SANCTUARY OF
POMPEI », but as follows; « HISTORY, MIRACLES
AND NOVENA OF THE MOST BLESSED VIRGIN OF THE
ROSARY OF POMPEI BY BARTOLO LONGO, ESQ. »

We therefore intended to write a book for
the use of the pious, and it was for this reason
that, to the narrative of the miracles, we added,
in the form of a Novena, the prayer which we
had written purposely to render honor to our
Image of the Rosary. And in order to introduce
into the hearts of the faithful devotion toward
this sacred Effigy we placed at the beginning
of that History a hastily executed lithograph.
So that was the first book which appeared with
a picture of Our Lady of Pompei.

That first History comprised all the facts
and miracles that had taken place in the years
1876, 1877 and 1878.

The first edition of two-thousand copies having been exhausted in less time than I could
have supposed, that is within the space of twelve
months, I was obliged in 1880 to hastily com-
pile a second edition, which I committed to
the then existing printinghouse of the Fibreno

in Naples; and in order to satisfy the constantly increasing demands, within six-days a thousand other copies had already been printed. This second edition I enlarged somewhat by the addition of a few pages.

After the lapse of four months of the same year 1880, through the typography of Andrea and Salvatore Festa, we issued a third edition of threethousand copies, more voluminous than the preceeding, that is to say consisting of 144 pages, as it contained the extraordinary events of the year 1879.

But this third edition also was soon exhausted, and so in the month of May of the year 1881 we published a fourth one of four thousand copies, also through the Printing House of the Firm of Festa, and this we enriched with still other notices of the extraordinary events of the year 1880, thus making a volume of 224 pages.

The following year of 1882 we renewed the edition in the same type and shape and that was the fifth.

But already the devotion to the Virgin of the Rosary of Pompei had become diffused throughout the northern part of Italy: at the same time that Our Lady was granting special

graces in Tuscany, she was also working wonders in Milan, in Turin and in Venice. Hence
we were obliged in the course of one year, that
of 1883, celebrated in the annals of the New
Pompei, to undertake two editions; and these
were the sixth and seventh, again printed by
the Firm of Festa of Naples.

Then follows the year 1884, a year of hard
trials, but of still more glorious triumphs, as
will be seen by this History, whence the new
works of art, of beneficence and of civilization
originated, that are the cause of so much won-
derment to all who visit the Sanctuary. And
in the course of that year we published two
large editions, the eighth and the ninth, to the
number of twelve thousand copies, also printed
by the firm of Festa of Naples; and these were
the last published in Naples.

In the year 1885 we had already started our
typography in Valle di Pompei, and so the tenth
and eleventh editions immediately appeared,
this time in our own types. But now we gave the
work a new title: « HISTORY OF THE GROWING
SANCTUARY OF POMPEI, DEDICATED TO THE QUEEN
OF THE HOLY ROSARY, BY BARTOLO LONGO, ESQ. »
And as all preceeding editions had been
scarce, despite the abundant number of copies,

*we did not hesitate then to give to the light
full sixteen thousand examplaries.*

*Thenceforth we published no further editions
of the History, as our Periodical, entitled:
« THE ROSARY AND THE NEW POMPEI », contains
every month, as the events take place, a detailed
account of all that concerns the Sanctuary and
the new-born Pompei.*

*To-day we give to the light not a new edi-
tion of the old History, but on the contrary
a new History. New, not only as regards the
chronicling of the events transpired in the course
of fourteen years, that is from 1881 to 1895, e-
vents of which the former Histories could make
no mention, but also as regards more minute par-
ticulars concerning primitive events, to which
before we had attached no importance, but which
later facts have proven to us to have been not
only of importance but also worthy of note.
And besides this, the character of that former
work jotted down more as a compendium, and
intended merely to inflame the hearts of people,
did not consent to our indulging in minutiae.
In those editions moreover, through natural modesty and not foreseeing the future, I concealed
both my name and that of the Countess De Fusco,
under the identity of « Some Tertiaries of*

Saint Dominic » *a title of wich we were, and are, proud.*

But the manner of writing is also different in this new work: for, having set before my mind, as in a synthesis, the history of the fifteen years that I have undertaken to write, I have with greater care sought for the inner reason of certain facts, and have thus exposed in cronological order events, which before I had related singly, and I have also put them in juxta-position with other facts, however slight, yet essential, that Providence has made use of to carry on the work committed to our humble cares.

And lastly the title also is new: « HISTORY OF THE SANCTUARY OF POMPEI »; *because it is the first time that a complete History of the Sanctuary from its first beginnings up to the present time has been presented to the public.*

For all these various reasons I heartily hope that this my humble work may turn out to be of great use to all classes of persons and of still greater honor to the Most Blessed Virgin.

INTRODUCTION

Having received from Heaven not one, but innumerable benefits, and not least among these, that of a life preserved, through the intercession of our great Mother, whom we venerate in Pompei by her title of the Rosary, I could not fail to realize my great debt of gratitude, and I felt my heart burn with an immense desire to love and praise Mary, and lead others also to love and praise her. From the very moment that this loving Mother showed herself so merciful unto me, it became my firm purpose to consecrate my life to her service and to the propagation of her worship, and especially of the divine Rosary, so acceptable unto Her: hence arose my intention of spending yearly five hundred francs of my own to raise a simple altar on this abandoned plain, around which to gather the simple country folk in order to instruct them in the recital of the Rosary.

The events have surpassed my intention. It was only when I beheld the blessing of

God descending so abundantly on my humble efforts, that I first planned to raise a Throne to Our Lady of such beauty and religious attractiveness, as to draw the faithful here to venerate Her on this spot.

Nor yet could I oppose any obstacle to the designs of the Lord, when suddenly I found myself in the midst of such unusual and prodigious events, that it was simply impossible for me to explain: and when day after day I received letters bearing testimony to benefits received, telling of health miraculously recuperated and of innumerable and extraordinary graces bestowed at the invocation of the Virgin of Pompei; it appeared to me that there was no better way to choose, than to second what Providence itself was working out; and what it has done, everyone sees.

But in order that even those who are distant, and cannot themselves come to Valle di Pompei to behold the great works of the Lord, may join together with us to exalt our Mother, and invoke Her aid with faith and efficacy, I have had to go a step further; namely I have been obliged to reach the determination to render Her a still greater honor, by narrating the various facts, some of them mayhap very insignificant in the eyes of the world, which, containing in themselves as they do the germ of a development superior to any human prevision, have been the origin of events of a most extraordinary nature. But not only have I wished to narrate them with that conscientious veracity and exactness required by history, precisely as persons worthy of belief have referred them to us and as we have beheld them with our own eyes, but I have also wished to study them deeply knowing as I well do, that the works of God, in their eloquent language, are at once simple and profound.

And here I find it my duty to confess that in the study of these facts I have found a link, a superior principle, an agent of infinite perfection which connects and binds them, a starting point, on which, as Dante Alighieri says:

Heaven and all Nature do depend.

This truth I have sought to instill into the minds of my readers. And it appears to me that a History of the Sanctuary of Pompei, written with this criterion, must answer the demands not only of those who read to satisfy their religious appetite, admiring the works of God; but also of those believers who still feel the need of an accurate research of the truth in order to glorify Him.

Certainly, if one consider the incessant stream of visitors of all classes and conditions, of pilgrims, of men of note, of Bishops and of those high in authority in the Church, and State, of entire religious communities, who undertake long journeys, from all points of the compass, to come and pray before an altar raised on a spot wholly unknown fifteen years ago, in fact dreaded, until a short while since by travellers, as a resort of thieves and vagabonds, and now changed suddenly into a renowned Sanctuary; if one behold the vast edifice here raised by the faith of so many peoples of divers tongues, and that will cost no less than two millions; one cannot help being struck by a profound admiration, and stimulated not only to examine the proofs of all supernatural events adduced, but also to investigate in what manner and by which logical connection of things and ideas, this faith has become spread abroad on all sides.

How has this come to pass? How came such a fact to be possible in this our nineteenth century, in which the broad and sincere faith of the Middle Ages has no hold?

This is a question that will be put by many.

To answer it I have not felt the need of allowing myself to be guided by too impetuous a zeal, and much less by that certain fanaticism of which ofttimes prejudiced and over-clouded minds accuse catholic writers: but I have with a cool and accurate disquisition, strengthened by testimonies and by the evidence of facts and of Faith, narrated that, which every man who does not willfully desire to deny the light that triumphantly appears, must in good conscience affirm with sure asseverance. And this have I done without aught adding or aught hiding, but simply following the pure and full truth.

The duke of Saint-Simon was wont to say, that when he wrote he shut his door to men and told a story that was to be confided to a century.

I have written these pages in my little study, situated in the first room contiguous to the Sanctuary of our beloved Mother of Pompei; from this room I behold the summit of Mount Gauro, made memorable by the apparition of the Archangel Saint Michael to Saint Catello, Bishop of Castellammare. In the silence that reigns in wintertime in this valley, it has ofttimes seemed to me that I was alone in the midst of a desert world. And at the sight of the lovely azure sky above me, and at the contemplation of that mount which constantly recalls to my mind the celestial apparition and the angelic colloquy, it has seemed to me, while writing, that I too, far from speaking to mortals of this earth, was conversing with beings who soar through the infinitude of space. To them have I confided my simple tale, and thus do I give it to the press.

Every lover of truth will find means to convince himself of its presence here.

I have quoted names, domiciles and witnesses, because as the persons are yet living, they may be questioned; and so the reader, having thus convinced himself of the veracity of my recital, will also bear testimony to the truth. Nevertheless there are men who love darkness better than light; and for this reason am I sure that the History of the Sanctuary of Pompei will find two species of contradictors.

The first will be that of the sceptics, or free thinkers, who hearing a History interwoven with miracles and supernatural events, will shrug their shoulders and smile derisively, and laugh at our credulity, which they will term superstition; and so will with a very easy and convenient method deny every thing.

With such as these we will undertake no reasoning or dispute, as their manner of getting out of a difficulty is by systematically denying everything. Instead we invite them, not to read this History, but to come to Valle di Pompei, and they will have to believe their own eyes. In fact several have come, have seen, and have believed in a divine Providence that regulates events in this spot in a manner wholly supernatural.

The other class of contradictors is that composed of christians, or rather of false christians, who enjoy contradicting, sometimes because of their frivolity and sometimes because incapable of governing their love of slander; and forgetting the great saying of the Redeemer: *Nolite judicare ut non iudicemini*; « judge not that ye be not judged,» often pronounce the most inconsiderate verdicts, often producing a greater harm than they themselves suspected. This is a class much to be feared as they appear to speak for the love of truth.

But this class is complex; those who speak in good faith either oppose or curse the work of God, because they hear others, in whom they blindly trust, do the same; and without searching for the truth themselves they do as the sheep of whom the Poet wrote:

« *And as the one, so too the others do* ».

For such as these this History will be of use, as it will at least serve to more seriously call the attention of their conscience and of their judgment to this work and move them to see and examine if what we state is true.

Those of bad faith belong to the evil seed of Juda and to the priests of the old law who killed Jesus thinking thus to do a thing that would be pleasing in the sight of God.

For these there is no other hope than the mercy of Mary to enlighten and convert them. And for these too do we pray.

BOOK FIRST
The Ancient Valley of Pompei.

CHAPTER I.

Ancient and modern Pompei.

The traveller who wishes, in the space of a few hours, to visit the Sanctuary that rises in honor of the Virgin of the Rosary on this « *piece of Heaven fallen to Earth* », as the poets called this perivesuvian zone, needs but to present himself at the station of Naples and ask for a return ticket for Valle di Pompei, the next stopping place after Pompei. The whole trip takes but sixty-five minutes.

What a delightful road! The beautiful sea as clear and blue as the sky it reflects, is never lost sight of during the whole trip and it lies rippling and dazzling to the right of the railroad track.

First he passes along the open, broad sea beach, after which he leaves to the left smiling

Portici, Resina, the ancient Herculanum and Oplonto, once sisters in mourning to Stabia and to Pompei, and over which, like a giant on guard, ever towers grand old Vesuvius, with his high crest of smoke.

To the right his eye wanders across the broad gulf, ever further, ever further, till arrested by the mountains that rear themselves immediately behind Castellammare; then slowly shifting his gaze toward the poetical shores of fair Sorrento, that ever recall to mind the sweet Singer of Goffredo, immortal Tasso, he beholds, lost in the blue azure of the distance, as though hung between sea and sky, Point Minerva.

But already the scene has changed; Torre del Greco, the city of corals, twelve times rebuilt by its inhabitants who have ever pertinaceously returned to the ruins of their city covered by the lava of Vesuvius, obstinate enemy of spirits still more obstinate in the love of their native soil, has been passed on the left. And so too has Torre Annunziata, flourishing in its commerce and industries been left behind. The train now stops at the Station of ancient Pompei; but the Valley of the Sanctuary has not yet been reached.

As yet, though the traveller is wholly
intent on going directly to venerate the great
Mother of God in her monumental temple,
nevertheless hearing the conductor call out
— Pompei, — he almost unconsciously looks
out of the window; a thousand indistinct,
confused ideas, of antiquity, of history, of
paganism and of ruin, rush simultaneously
to his mind.

Pompei! Magic, historical word, that attracts
the attention and the study of all earth's cultured men. Pompei, splendid and majestic
among all the etruscan cities that vaunted
Capua for their metropolis! Seneca and Tacitus,
Florus and Titus Livius called her fair and
flourishing, because of the beauty of her sky
the activity of her commerce and the importance of her communications. Softly reclining
on velvety hills, she rested her head on the
side of a mountain of fire; fountains of pure
water, flowing forth from the Sarno, refreshed
her bosom, and at her feet, in calm repose,
lay the smiling gardens, and the fertile plains,
irrigated by the waters of that historic river,
in those days navigable.

But that mountain vomited devouring flames;
destruction rained and poured from its heaving

sides, burying every grandeur in its train;
and over that immense hecatomb, like a func-
real pall, was thrown a sheet of ashes.

The traveller sees but a huge mound of earth
and lapillae, that once buried a whole generation of living beings beneath their, pitiless
weight. And, scarce noticing that the train
is already moving along, he gazes on the
long stretch of walls, of roofless and ruined
dwellings, sees columns, some still entire and
standing, others broken and fallen, pass rapidly before his view; intermingled with the
remains of broken vaults and the ruins of
painted walls; till he sights the amphitheatre,
once given over to the spectacle of human
butcheries.

Unconsciously his brows contract; and
almost unknown to himself he has become
sad and pensive.

His thoughts have reverted back to the life,
habits and habitations of a people long since
extinct; roman spectres seem to wander about
those heights. From the contemplation of those
stones, still standing after a lapse of eighteen
centuries, his imagination descends to the
deserted streets, to that intricate web of long,
narrow, melancholy alleys. There is still the

road paved with vesuvian stones, shaped like
trapezoids, there still the cobble-stone side-
walk, there still the marks of the heavy carts
and vehicles upon the pavements; the houses
and the shops, the edifices and vast temples
still seem to await the return of their masters.
The fountains and statues, the paintings and
the exercise grounds of the aristocratic youth,
the tombs, the mosaics, porticos, theatres,
and amphitheatre, all speak of the roman
grandeur.

But the masters returned no more; all that
splendor came to an end. That pagan grandeur
did not go beyond the tomb, and nought did it
know of the future destinies of the human race.
Mute are the Forum, the public baths and the
temple of Apollo, mute the Pantheon, the temple
of Augustus, the two theatres and the vast
amphitheatre. Eighteen centuries of silence
lie heavy on them.

.·.

Five minutes have not passed and the sharp
whistle of the locomotive reminds the traveller that he has left the station of the
Pompei that is no more, and is approaching
that of the Pompei which is rising.

The scene as if by enchantment has changed. A svelte and elegant cupola appears a long way off. After the cupola, brilliant with light and displaying its variagated white and black checks, appears an immense building, distending itself along the side of the Sanctuary; then in front come other minor edifices, till the eye travelling further and further on beholds a straight road, an avenue shaded by a quadruple row of plantains and eucalyptus, that starts from a marble column, a mile stone, that bears the legend: VIA SACRA; and now finally he has reached the station of Valle di Pompei.

His foot has scarce touched ground, before the solemn sound of a bell reaches his ear. Those slow vibrations, resounding through the valley, extend the tremolo of their sonorous waves of sound far into the desert streets of the mute city. The christian's heart can scarce repress its vehement palpitations at such new and unexpected impressions.

By the side of a land of death he has suddenly come upon a land of resurrection and of life: instead of an Amphitheatre, stained with blood, he beholds a Temple alive with faith and love, a Temple sacred to the Mother Maid;

opposite a city, dead in pagan debauchery, throbs a new chaste and noble life, that takes its origin from the *New Civilization*, introduced by christianity: The new Pompei!

The eighteen centuries of silence hovering over those tombs are broken by that sacred toll; and the secular melancholy of that spot is gladdened by the tender song of children, by the little Orphans of the Rosary who from within the pale of the Sacred Arc praise the Lord. It is the new civilization by the side of the old, modern art by the side of ancient, that is here clearly to be observed; christianity, the source of life, face to face with paganism, whose sun has set forever.

But this singular confrontation of life and death on the selfsame soil becomes still more evident as soon as the threshold of the Sanctuary has been crossed. Here the glory of modern christian and italian painting and sculpture shines forth in its full splendor.

Those colored marbles of perfect workmanship, of incomparable hue and lustre, those frescoes of the Cupola, of the Apsis, and of the entire ceiling of the Sanctuary, the angels that form a crown all around the upper part of the church, those finely worked statues of bronze and marble; that wealth of gilding throughout the vast edifice, that wondrous softness of tints, that perfection of christian art in purest tuscan style; all these are eloquent voices that loudly speak to the heart of the traveller, and to the mind of every lover of art and of religion saying: Here the new art has succeeded to the old; the new civilization has supplanted the ancient; here christianity triumphs over paganism.

All this great movement of life and art, of civilization and of religion, did not exist here eleven years ago. All this splendor that bursts on the sight of the visitor like a sweet vision after the dark and melancholy thoughts of death and ruin, had no existence but a few years ago.

.·.

And here the traveller will want to know how so rapid a change, that must of a necessity seem an exageration to the distant and appears as a dream even to those who are present, came to pass.

To satisfy this just desire I must however begin far back, and reveal the earliest origin of this great phenomenon. But prior to beginning these researches, it appears to me wise and reasonable to premit a few truths, that will place my narrative in a more evident light.

1. The work of Pompei is the work of God! The Virgin Mary is directing it to His glory. and the means of promulgation, of which She avails Herself, are miracles!

In this work is hidden a profound and secret design of God, not yet fully developed. And when God *wills* a thing, be men willing or not, it is sure to be accomplished.

This much we can asseverate, without fear of erring, that it surely is a *design of mercy*.

However we must confess that we ourselves were at first mistaken because of our lack of understanding of the divine signs. We thought in the beginning that they were but designs of mercy to be shown to the poor country folk of this Valley; and we blindly followed the impulse, that we felt within us to instruct and benefit merely the ignorant people of the country roundabout. But with the lapse of years, with the unceasing multiplying of the prodigies of our heavenly Queen, with the centuplication of letters of foreigners and of strangers from the most remote regions of the world, who turn to us either to thank the Virgin for benefits received, or to ask for new favors; with the coming hither of so many illustrious personages and church and state authorities, so that oftentimes our shoulders can scarce bear so heavy a load, and still we behold a *constant increase, a steady progress,* we have at last become aware of the fact that God's design is one of mercy yes, but not of partial, but of *universal mercy.*

2. If the work of Pompei is the work of God, it must needs be *constantly opposed.* The gospel comforts us and teaches us that our Redeemer was the First to be placed as a sign that should be contradicted: Signum in quo contradicetur, *Contradiction* is the distinguishing sign of all His works. *This is the surest sign that your work is the work of God*, thus spake to us one day the greatest personage of our times, the High Pontiff Leo XIII, *because you suffer contradiction; but the Virgin will cause your work to triumph.* And in fact as will be seen by this History, there has not been a triumph of the Sanctuary that was not preceded by a battle, nor a glory not preceded by a humiliation.

Thus will our reader see how constantly all our great consolations have only come after

great bitterness, and that in all our arduous
trials we have been sustained and strengthened
by the loving hand of the Mistress of this
Valley, whose title is the Queen of Victories.

3. In this work of Pompei Providence incon-
trovertably manifests itself; that Providence
so often denied or cursed in these days.

Without any sure income, without any sur-
plus, without any fixed capital; without any
help from city or state government, thousands
of francs are spent weekly, and hundreds of
families, workmen, children and orphans are
daily supported. On Saturday evening not a
cent remains. But on the following Saturday
the money is there, ready and forthcoming and
this has been going on for *twelve* years; and
we have in this manner succeeded in disbur-
sing more than *three million* francs! — Who
can doubt that there exists a Providence?

4. From facts, in which I myself have either
been an actor, or of which I have been and
still am a witness, as I will show, it will
be easy for everyone to conclude *that there
is not a sinner so lost, but he may find safety
in the Rosary of Mary.* There is not a soul,
however bound and chained by Satan, that
cannot break loose from its bonds, by holding

on to that chain of refuge, which the Queen of Heaven extends from above for the salvation of the shipwrecked in life's tempestuous sea.

5. To triumphantly carry on even the most difficult and arduous works undertaken for the honor of God, there is no need either of *riches*, of *power*, or of *wisdom*. When all things are done as ordained and with sincere faith, for all the rest one thing alone, that draws from Heaven the full abundance of superhuman help, is necessary, and that is — *a right intention.*

———

CHAPTER II.

The Ancient Valley of Pompei.

§ 1.

THE INEXPLORED VALLEY.

Prior to beginning this historical narrative, it seems to me to be a wise plan to premit a brief notice regarding the spot where the events chronicled in this sketch have taken place.

If the building of a new city and of a monumental Temple, (erected in the shortest possible time in an open and abandoned country), that like a magnet attracts the heart of so many inhabitants of this globe, is a remarkable fact; then too is it important to know what this spot, chosen by Providence, in this century of ours, so prone to deny Providence, as the theatre of its portents, was in times gone by; and what it is to day now that the Queen of Angels has chosen it as the seat of Her Throne of mercies.

To whosoever comes from the amphitheatre of Pompei, continues on his way toward

Scafati, and lets his eyes roam over the surrounding country, a most beautiful valley pre-
sents itself; this valley, lying to the southward
of Mount Vesuvius, is irrigated to the right
and to the left by two rivers, the Sarno and
the Canal of the Sarno, and, fertil and rich
in various annual productions, it lies smiling
for many miles round about the solitary ruins.

A long chain of mountains, a spur projec-
ting from the Appenines, forms from east to
south a broad and ample belt round about.
They are the same mountains that hedge in
the Valley of the Sarno, lengthen themselves
out toward Amalfi, and then finishing the
circle, tower, towards the south, above Castellammare di Stabia, till with a long arm
they stretch themselves down to the sea at
the Point of Sorrento or as it is often called
the Point of the Campanella.

Thus crowned by her mountains, covered
for the most part with a luxuriant vegetation
of olive and of chestnut trees, and brimming
over with life teaming in numberless beautiful
villages that nestle on their summits or their
slopes; this valley reposes proudly between
two neighboring mountains that give her
renown and historic fame: these are, to the

north, Vesuvius, that with its menacing crater,
and rough, rugged sides, stands directly over
her like a lord and master, and Mount Gauro
to the south, that, with its three dark peaks,
covered with fruit bearing woods and olive-
trees, watches over her like a protector or a
sentinel on guard.

This spot, to-day strewn with farm-houses,
buildings and villas, that day by day in increasing numbers cluster around the growing
Sanctuary of the Rosary, numbered at the beginning of the present century but a few souls:
and to day thanks to the movement of life
and art, of all of which the rising Temple and
the works instituted by us are the origin, it
numbers more than three thousand.

This Valley has to-day become famous, not
through the antiquity of the destroyed pagan
city, or the number of visitors curious to behold ancient monuments, but in truth through
the marvels here done by the blessed Virgin
by means of her new Temple dedicated to the
Rosary; and through the concourse of numberless illustrious pilgrims who flock hither
from every city and every clime, to venerate
Her who is the Queen of graces and of mercies
and Consoler of the afflicted.

But what was once this valley that to day
has become the centre of the affection of
hundreds of thousands of faithful? What was
its name in bygone days? What its history,

« *In the days of false and lieing Gods?* »

∴

During the course of all the centuries that
have elapsed since the year of our Lord
seventy-nine, year in which Pompei was destroyed, to the present day, that, which we
now call Valley of Pompei, was unknown,
or we had perhaps better say, unexplored.
Even in the writings of the learned we find
no mention of it.

Should one of our readers even to-day
question students of antiquity and ask them:

— What became of the country, lying to the
east and south of ancient Pompei, after the
year *seventy-nine?* Whither went the dispersed
Pompeians after the day of the fatal destruction
of their beloved city?

Their answer would be: — It is hard to say.

The fact is no one could ever have imagined
that this obscure, unknown, unstudied Valley,

had been so called ever since the remotest antiquity, and that the name it to-day bears of Valle di Pompei is its own by historic right.

Who could ever have supposed that this abandoned spot chosen by Mary as a centre of her portents in this nineteenth century, could have had the historical importance it did, not only in the time when ancient Pompei was at the height of its glory, but also in the middle centuries, from the XI to the XVII.

We have therefore been doubly fortunate! we have given birth, with the new Sanctuary raised in honor of the Queen of the Rosary, to a new town, that may become the *New Pompei,* not only, but we have also found the key that unlocks the door to a better knowledge of the historical importance of this Valley dear to Mary. The way we came to make this important discovery was very simple.

In 1887, in order to prepare for the triumph of the blessed Virgin in this valley, on that ever memorable day of the eighth of May, day in which She was to take possession of her throne in Pompei, we not only built, on ground belonging to us, a small station, bearing the name of Valle di Pompei for the greater convenience of all visitors to this Sanctuary, we

not only opened through the fields of the
De Fusco family an avenue leading from said
Station to the Sanctuary, avenue which we
called *Via Sacra*, but we also, at our own
expense, made a square, at one extremity of
which we began to dig the foundations of a
model modern Workingmen's Home. When lo
and behold, while digging the foundations,
some ruins appear; proceeding carefully the
laborers came upon ancient rooms, and upon
monuments, of the Pompeian epoch.

These, having been studied by the famous
archaeologist Ludovico Pepe, were the cause
of his writing the history of this Valley from
the first century of the christian era up to
the present day; and this history is enriched
and sustained by incontrovertible documents
found by rummaging among the old parchments
hidden in the diocesian archives, as well as
in those of the various libraries and notorial
files [1]).

Following therefore the revelations afforded
by the monuments discovered by us, and the

---

[1]) See HISTORICAL MEMOIRS OF THE ANCIENT OF VALLEY
OF POMPEI by *Ludovico Pepe*. Valle di Pompei, Editing
School of Typography of Bartolo Longo 1887.

studious and learned researches brilliantly
concluded by the very distinguished archaeologist Ludovico Pepe, we are glad to offer
to the reader of the History of the Sanctuary
of Pompei, a brief epilogue of eighteen centuries of history in this valley, till yesterday
abandoned and forgotten by all, but chosen
by Providence unto the glory of the Virgin,
for the moral and civil resurrection of this
pompeian people, and for the increase and
spread of faith so rapidly decreasing in the
world.

§ 2.

THE ANCIENT VALLEY IN THE FIRST CENTURY.

What was the Valley of Pompei in the days
in which pagan Pompei flourished?

The valley we to-day call Valley of Pompei
was in the times of the ancient city called
Campus Pompeianus. It was crossed by roads
that from Pompei led to Stabia, to Nocera
and to other important towns in the Valley
of the Sarno; and it was also intersected by
roads that from this spot led to the above-
named cities; for this reason, besides all agri-
cultural, city industries also, could freely

prosper here. Rustic villas, manifacturies and shops adorned the outlying country, rich in luxuriant vegetation.

But what was the state of this Valley after the eruption?

When the city and its surroundings had been buried beneath the ashes and lapillae, and all around remained mute and desolate, a ray of life appeared on the spot nearest the Amphitheatre, on the very site of our excavations, that began on the western side of the large square we opened in *New Pompei*.

Here, on top of the ancient monuments we found the tombs of those who had lived there after the eruption; these tombs we found excavated in the ashes, and built on the lapillae erupted in the year 79. They are tombs, for the poor, prepared without show and proving that those who built them were obliged to content themselves with what they could get. They are pagan tombs; in them were found the ointment boxes, the lamps placed at the feet of the body, all of which objects we have collected and preserved. The constructions which we found, built on top of the ancient ones, are the work of the new inhabitants of the valley.

A still more evident indication of this important discovery was a piece of brass money of the Emperor Diocletian, found in a room built against some ancient walls, that belonged to an epoch greatly anterior to the eruption. The Roman Emperor Diocletian lived in the third century; therefore the occupants of this house must have lived there at least until the fourth century, as we have found monuments belonging to that century that most evidently prove the valley to have been inhabited.

We again find this valley mentioned in the ninth century by the name of Campus Pompeianus, by the chronicler Martino Monaco, who in the History of the transfer of the body of Saint Bartholomew from Lipari to Benevento tells that Sicardo, prince of Benevento, for fear that the Saracens might attempt a disembarkment, had encamped his army, anno 838 *in Pompeio Campo, qui a Pompeja, urbe Campaniae, nunc deserta, nomen accepit.*

Campus Pompeianus it was therefore called in the IX century, from the name of the destroyed city of *Pompei in Campania.* At anyrate, whether *Campo* or *Valle,* it takes its name from *Pompeja.*

It may be for this reason that the old curate
of Valle, Don Giovanni Cirillo, who has died
within the last year, took for the motto to be
engraven on his seal the words « Parish of the
most holy Saviour in the ancient land of Valle
a Pompeja, » as we will narrate.

§ 3.

THE SACRED VALLEY.
THE FIRST POMPEIAN CHRISTIANS.

Here very naturally one's curiosity might
be aroused to know whether among the first
inhabitants of Valle di Pompei, there were
any converts to the christian faith.

We will satisfy this desire by stating that
in the ancient destroyed city not even the
slightest vestige of christianity was found;
and that for this reason the Valley of Pompei,
inhabited by idolatrous Pompeian fugitives,
remained for a long time in the darkess of
paganism.

The ray of new civilization that had together with christianity penetrated Naples and
Rome and nearly all Italy, watered by the
blood of martyrs, was very late in illumining

the minds of the descendants of that city, so famous for its luxury and gentile voluptuousness, and whose ruins to this day bear the impress of dissoluteness and depravity.

We must reach the fourth century in order to find the first traces of christianity in Pompei.

It is true that in the excavations of Pompei there was found a lamp with the sign of the cross: but Father Garrucci of the S. O. J. in his *Pompeian Questions* recognized in that cross signed lamp certain distinguishing features of the fourth century; that is to say of those same inhabitants whom Fiorelli and all archaeologists declare to belong to the third and fourth centuries. These inhabitants were wont to go and dig within the ruins of ancient Pompei, and by making apertures in the upper part of the houses, they entered them and carried off everything of value. Some of them however, after having penetrated through the apertures, remained buried within and were suffocated by the falling of lapillae and of ruins. And thus is explained the presence of a christian lamp of the fourth century among the excavations of Pompei.

Neither have we found in the vast edifice, brought to light by us, any trace of christianity.

But certainly those same christians of the IV century, who inhabited that part of the valley excavated by us, were the progenitors of those Pompeians who built the church of the *Most Holy Saviour* on the banks of the river Sarno not quite a mile distant from the unearthed « *fullonica* ». The first time we find that church mentioned by any writer is in the year 1093.

It can therefore with safety be asserted that after the destruction of Pompei a hamlet was built in the underlying valley, and along the banks of the river Sarno, in those days navigable, and this hamlet, taking its name from the situation in which it was built (that is in the lower part, along the river) was called Valle. And here a church in honor of the Most Holy Saviour was erected. Around this church the dispersed inhabitants of all the valley gathered, and thus formed the new city [1]).

According to the principles of the philosophy of history given us by Vico, of the flux and reflux of generations and of various epochs, we would call to the notice of the reader a singular fact that as the formation of the city

---

[1]) See PEPE, loc. cit.

of Valle was begun by the building of a church
around which the first inhabitants gathered;
so in this our century around the church of the
Rosary the scattered dwellers in the modern
valley are clustering, thus to form a new city.

And if the Sanctuary that to-day rises in
our midst is of great importance, even socially
considered, of no less importance was the
Church of the new Pompeian Christians.

In fact it is to be seen, according to Pepe,
that in 1093 the ancient church of Valle became an *Abbey*, it having been given by the
Bishop of Nola, Sassone, to Hugo, Abbot of
the Benedictine monks of Aversa [1].

In 1215 we find it mentioned in the Brief:
« *In eminenti Apostolicæ Sedis* » of the High
Pontiff Innocent III. From this we learn that
the Abbey of Valle extended from the sea to
Vesuvius, and to the east as far as the Sarno [2].

---

[1] See the important Diploma of the first half of
the XIV Century found by PEPE in the grand Archives of Naples. Reg. 165. ROBERTUS 1310. C. Fol. 257 t.

[2] This Brief dated from the Lateran, March 18, 1215
nineteenth year of the Pontificate of Innocent III,
describes the confines of the Diocese of Nola, keeping
sight of those already determined by Alexander III
(1159-1181) and by Celestin III (1191-1198).

It was in 1337 that this rich Abbey-Church of Valle, in the Campus Pompeianus, became poor and dowerless; when those same Benedictine monks of Aversa ceded *the Church and the town of Valle* and the property of the Church to Bernardo Caracciolo, in permutation, which possessions from that day formed the feud of the noble family of the Caracciolo of Naples.

Caracciolo enjoyed the benefit of these possessions, but the church became exceedingly impoverished, whence the citizens of the *University of Valle*, in the XVI century, decided to endowe it; but from that time it reentered the jurisdiction of the Bishop of Nola. However the ancient citizens of Valle, as far back as 1511, thus acquired the so-called right of *Patronage*, which was to present to the Bishop of Nola the nominee for the pastorship.

Even to this day the Parish of the Most Holy Saviour in Valle di Pompei is one of the *only eighteen parishes* in Italy, in which the right of electing the pastor by the voice of the people is in full vigor. What a singular Valley this is!

Pepe however has good reason to doubt the authenticity of the Bull of Julius II, of the

year 1511, with which this right of popular
election is conferred for the first time, and that
to the people of Valle. He suspects it to be
apocryphal, as he has not yet been able to find
in the Archives at Rome the said Bull, not
even among such of them as are printed. Moreover he finds it to be identical to another
Bull sent to the citizens of Bologna. But we
commit the care of the research as to the truth
in this matter to the Diocesian Authority, a
watchful guardian of all ecclesiastical rights.

§ 4.

THE VALLEY OF POMPEI THE THEATRE OF WAR IN THE MIDDLE AGES.

The land of Valle is mentioned in the Middle
Ages not only because of its church, as we
have seen, but also because of its Castle, Feud,
and township, with its Municipality, or University, and with its Mayors.

From documents found in the Grand Archives of Naples, in the National Library of the
same city and in the important Archives of
the episcopal See of Nola, where the accounts
of the Holy Visits made by the pastors in those

times are still preserved, it is clear to see that the township of Valle was well inhabitated and guarded by a *castle,* more important than the one of Scafati. And in occasion of the historical *conspiracy of the Barons ,* promoted by the prince of Taranto against Ferdinand the First of Aragon this Valley rises into importance.

Not far distant from here, near the town of Sarno , Ferdinand came to battle with the Anjoin forces, that were strengthened by the troops of the conspiring Barons. The famous defeat of Sarno fell to the lot of Ferdinand.

The following day, as is known in History, the Anjoin army went to Castellammare di Stabia, passing through our territory of Valle [1]).

Meanwhile it came to pass that in the year 1459, Louis Caracciolo, the great feudal lord of our Valle, took the side of the Barons in the famous conspiracy.

But Ferdinand, protected by Pope Pius the second, a Piccolomini , and coadjuvated by Anthony Piccolomini, a nephew of the Pope, routed the army of the Barons; took the

---

[1]) See Documents taken from the national library in Naples, manuscript signed IX C. XXIII, fol. 209, (in possession of PEPE).

rebellious Louis Caracciolo prisoner, pardoned him his life, but took from him the feud of Valle, which he gave to his faithful N. Toraldo.

In 1550 the feud of Valle was by Toraldo sold to Jacob of the Bucchis, from whose hands it passed into those of Alphonse Piccolomini who bought the entire feud of Valle, that is *the Castle, the houses, the Palace of the University, the men, the vassals, and all the feudal rights;* whence later he received the title of Prince of Valle [1]).

Because of these things our Valley was in 1647 elevated to the dignity of a *principality* [2]).

§ 5.

DESTRUCTION OF THE ANCIENT TOWNSHIP OF VALLE IN THE SEVENTEENTH CENTURY.

But when and how was the ancient Terra di Valle destroyed?

The Prince of Valle, Alphonse Piccolomini, in order to draw the water of the Sarno to

---

[1]) PEPE loc. cit.

[2]) The Piccolomini held it till the beginning of this century, that is up to 1818, in which year the noble family became extinct, and it passed into the hands of the De Fusco.

put in motion the mills he owned in Scafati
and in Torre, caused enormous palisades and
long dykes to be built, which in a short time
produced an overflow of the river. Thus not
only did navigation become impossible, but
the overflown waters having collected into
pools, and having become stagnant, with pes-
tiferous exhalations, the air soon became fatal
to all the populations of Sarno, of Nocera, of
Scafati, of Striano, of San Pietro, of San Va-
lentino, of Angri and of other towns. An enormous palisade, the most fatal of all, and a
dyke of 950 palms, were near the Church of
the Most Holy Saviour and from that church
took their name.

Hence from that day the inhabitants began
to decrease, partly on account of the mor-
tality and partly on accout of emigration. In
vain did the poor, suffering communities go
to law and obtain favorable sentences, the
Prince of Valle, with the usual highhanded-
ness of feudal Barons constituted himself
superior to the law.

With such a decrease of citizens, the hearths
in the University of Valle became scarcer and
scarcer in number, till the terrible and famous
pest of 1656 mowed down the last victims,

leaving intact but three families, whose descendants are still living.

But the complete abandonment of the Town of Valle is to be placed in the year 1659 [1]). After three years, that is to say in 1662, the ancient Parish was reduced to a simple benefice, by decree of the Bishop of Nola in his episcopal visit of that year. But that Bishop, Monsignor Conzaga, perhaps because so inspired by Heaven, placed at the foot of said Decree the following lines: Should the inhabitants of Valle in the future reach the number of *fifteen*, this church is to be reintegrated in its rights and is to have the care of souls.

That clause, seemingly of so slight importance, enclosed the germ of the resurrection of a dead city.

---

[1]) See *Process* of the Archives of Nola. Vol. II Docum. 1762 (in possession of Pepe).

CHAPTER III.

The Valley after its destruction.

THE DISMEMBERED VALLEY.

And so the inhabitants who were not killed by the deadly miasma or by the pestilence were scattered to distant parts. Many families settled down in the country round about the modern Valle, and built new dwellings, far away from the river, along the roads that lead to Ottajano and to Naples, taking advantage of the materials remaining from the demolished buildings of the ancient Casale.

Other families went to dwell with the populations of the near towns, that is to say of Torre Annunziata and of Boscoreale, (a city lying in the province of Naples), and of Scafati, that forms a part of the province of Salerno. This is the reason why a part of the *Terra di Valle* goes with Scafati, a part with Torre Annunziata, a part with Boscoreale; while, still another part, as far as ecclesiastical jurisdiction is concerned, is subject to the province of Terra di Lavoro, because in this latter province lies Nola. But however this happened only after the destruction of the Township and of the Parish of Valle.

In fact from the XI to the XVI century, in which period of time we find the Terra of Valle so often mentioned, in all of the documents we can discover no reference made to the Casale (or settled township), other than by the simple name of Valle, without any further designation.

And the historic reason for this is most evident. Before Torre Annunziata and Boscoreale, even before Scafati existed, Valle was a township, fully autonomous, with its Feud, and Castle, its Municipality or University, with its Mayors and Parish Priests.

— The township of Valle — the historian Giustiniani tells us was well populated, and had an entity all its own. — The territory, over which the Church had spiritual jurisdiction was as vast as is now that over which the Parishes of Torre Annunziata and of Boscoreale, of comparatively recent formation, have jurisdiction.

It is therefore evident that, in the second half of the XVII century, when the malarious air caused the obliteration of the township, a part of that district became incorporated in the Province of Salerno, and a part remained, as heretofore, in the province of Naples.

But in the year 1740, after the building of the ancient Parish of the Most Blessed Saviour of Valle, near the river, had been destroyed, the few inhabitants of the New Valle, together with the Parish Priest and the Bishop of Nola, who obtained the necessary decree from the sacred congregation of the Bishops and Regulars, rebuilt the new Parish of the Most Blessed Saviour of the Terra di Valle, in the district of Boscoreale in the Province of Naples, and precisely on the spot called Fossa di Valle (Ditch of Valle), to-day belonging to Torre Annunziata. And from that year we may date the beginning of a new epoch, which is that of the modern Valle di Pompei.

§ 2.

THE NAME OF THE MODERN VALLEY.

Having thus shown the distinction and the independence of the Feud of Valle as regards neighboring communes, not to mention the autonomy of the Parish of Valle, rebuilt on territory lying in the Province of Naples, let us now proceed to prove how very natural it was the title of Pompei should be given to the valley lying round about the ancient ruins.

On the testimony of the already mentioned chronicler of the IX century, Martino Monaco, we are informed that in the times following the destruction of Pompei, when the memory of the location of the ancient city still lasted in the minds of men, the valley, that stretched itself out at its feet, was known by the name of Campo Pompeiano. Nor could it have been otherwise. It was the celebrated name of Pompei that naturally gave rise to the adjective Pompeiano as applied to the surrounding fields; and there was no other inhabited spot that could have usurped the name.

Then, between the IX and the X centuries, all knowledge of the location of ancient Pompei, dissappeared completely from the memory of man. And when in the XI century a small church, dedicated to the Saviour, was here built, and round about the church a town, it was named Valle, on account of its position in a Valley, near the river Sarno, and so this appellation took the place of that of Pompei and of Campo Pompeiano.

Did the word Valle require a distinctive
adjective? In those days it was not necessary,
because the town of Valle was in itself important and autonomous; moreover neither
Scafati, nor Torre Annunziata, nor Boscoreale had as yet arisen. But even had they
wished to give a distinguishing title to the
township, they most certainly would have
called it Valle di Pompei had they known of
the ruins buried almost beneath their feet. —
It is evident — (thus concludes the above
mentioned Pepe) — that if the location of
Pompei had been known, the underlying
township, that touched the very outskirts of
the ancient city would without any doubt have
been called Valle di Pompei, as we have seen
it was named before Campo Pompeiano in
the year 838.

But the real keynote to the Valley is given
us by history and by the church there built,
and by public documents which go to prove
the truth of what we write. Thus, after the
charge of souls had been abolished there,
the ancient church of the Redeemer in Valle,
which was situated near the present Royal
Powder Magazine, remained standing till the
year 1740. In that year it was demolished, and

rebuilt a little more than a mile further off, opposite the ancient tavern of the Prince of Valle, to-day property of Count De Fusco, on the spot called Ditch of Valle (Fossa di Valle) in the province of Naples. This spot is the line of demarcation between the two provinces; because the Taverna di Valle, belonging to Count de Fusco, is comprised in the territory of Scafati in the province of Salerno; and the Parish of the Most Holy Saviour of Valle, opposite, in the territory of Torre Annunziata in the province of Naples.

It was these reasonable motives that induced Don Giovanni Cirillo, the first Parish Priest of this modern Valle, (a man well posted as to the first origin of his Parish, and who had read important documents and ancient inscriptions), to have a seal, to be placed on all public acts, papers, and parochial documents, engraved with the inscription: — Parish of the Most Holy Saviour in the ancient Land of Valle a Pompeia — as we have already stated. And the Valley is full of papers bearing that legend; all the present citizens have some of these documents, either as attestations of birth, or of baptism, or as certificates of marriage or of death, and the like.

To-day, after two centuries have elapsed since the destruction of the town and of the Parish, both town and Parish come to life again. The Parish, that was reinstated as far back as 1840, assumed, together with its ancient title of Parish of the Most Holy Saviour in Valle, also a part of its territory, which was divided among the three communes of two provinces. The township of Valle, whose resurrection began on the eighth day of May 1887, on the day of the Coronation of the Virgin of the Rosary, with its worldwide known Sanctuary, with its trade-schools and charitable institutions, with its Infant and Orphan Asylums, with its Post and Telegraph Offices, with its schools and workingmen's homes, with its own station, bearing the name of Valle di Pompei, shall it not also in this historic spot resume its ancient denomination?

This resurrected Parish, this newborn Commune, how should we have called it the first time that we wrote the History of this Sanctuary? How would the reader have called it?

In order to distinguish it from other places and towns of Italy that also bear the name of Valle we designated it by an historical adjective. It lies half way between Scafati and

Torre Annunziata, near the celebrated ruins
of Pompei, now no longer unknown, but discovered and unearthed more than a century
ago. Who would not be naturally inclined
to add the designation of Pompei to the word
Valle? This was the ancient Campo Pompeiano;
this must be the Valle of Pompei. And as Pompei stands above it, and as we have here, near
the Sanctuary, discovered monuments, tombs,
streets, and shops belonging to Pompei, who
is he who would call this Valley other than
Valle di Pompei?

Now the name of Valle di Pompei is already
established. The Parish Priest, Giovanni Cirillo, who died in 1887, was the first to call
his Parish that of Valle di Pompei. We also
in founding the celebrated Church of the
Rosary, around which a new generation is
clustering, so called it. And lastly it was so
called by the Government and the Depart-
ment of Mails and Telegraphs; so it was called
by the railroad society, so by the Direction of
Taxes of Scafati; the Notaries of Naples, of
Castellammare, of Boscoreale and of Scafati
so call it in their public instruments; so it
was called by the Bishop of Nola when
asking priviledges for it from the Holy See,

so also by the High Pontiff Leo XIII in **His**
Briefs and Rescripts in favor of the Sanctuary
of the Most Holy Rosary; so by all the scien-
tists composing the Italian and foreign **Me-**
teorological Societies in distinguishing from
others the meteoric-geodinamic-vulcanologi-
cal Observatory of Valle di Pompei; and last
of all the whole world that looks with wonder
and with faith towards this spot calls it by
no other name save that of Valle di Pompei.

§ 3.

THE PARISH AND THE TAVERN OF VALLE.

Having reached this point of our historical
researches, we must still dwell for a moment
on this Parish and Tavern of Valle, as it is
on this small plot of ground that all the
extraordinary events, we are about to relate,
have taken place.

The ancient settlement having been destroyed and the old church of the Saviour in
Valle near the river demolished in 1740, a
new parochial church was built about a mile
distant, (and precisely in the already mentioned
locality of the Ditch of Valle, opposite the

renowned Tavern of Valle), with the materials of the same and with the money obtained by the sale of a bell of the ancient bell-tower of Valle, which was sold in Boscoreale for 150 ducats.

At the beginning of this century, that is in 1840, the inhabitants of this valley having reached the number of 300 and more, it became incumbent on Monsignor Pasca then Bishop of Nola, to act upon the already mentioned Memorial of Monsignor Conzaga, who had, as our reader will remember, written — That if in future the inhabitants of this Valley should reach the number of *fifteen,* this church is to be reintegrated with the care of souls. — So Monsignor Pasca having heard that in this Valley people died forsaken and without sacraments, obtained by a royal decree in that same year of 1840 the reintegration of this Parish with the care of souls.

And so two years later, in 1842, according to their ancient right, the Pastor, in the person of Don Giovanni Cirillo of Boscoreale was elected by the voice of the people, with 161 votes; and he, who was the first Pastor of the modern valley, enters as hero upon the scenes our narrative will disclose.

. .

Let us now give a rapid glance at the Tavern
of Valle, which has been an incidental cause
in the events that have gradually unfolded
themselves in this Sanctuary.

This Tavern of Valle was a humble hostelry
for travellers, and was situated on the provincial road that from Naples leads to Salerno,
in the point where the two roads Naples-Salerno, and Valle-Ottaiano, cross each other,
in the feud of Valle, property of the Prince
of Valle, on the extreme confine of the Province of Salerno, and opposite the new Parish
of the Holy Saviour in Valle.

This Tavern we find mentioned for the first
time in the year 1695 [1]).

With an instrument dated February 19ᵗʰ 1815,
and made out by Thomas Marra, Notary, of
Naples, the Tavern of Valle was ceded and
assigned to the Prince of Valle, Francis Pignatelli.

The 23 of November 1815 Prince Pignatelli
sold it to Mr. Gabriel Prete of Naples.

---

[1]) Grand Archive, Case N. 1051, Piccolomini and
Valle Patrimonio.

And on the 19th of February 1827 Gabriel Prete in his turn sold it to Count Francis de Fusco by means of an instrument made out by Louis Mazzola, Notary, of Naples.

Count De Fusco in 1844 built a second apartment above the five rooms already existing, and added 54 acres of adjoining land, buying the same from Don Diego Genoino of Naples, Palatine Count.

His son and heir, Count Albenzio De Fusco, having acquired still other adjoining lands, died in 1864, leaving his wife Countess Marianna De Fusco, née Farnararo of Monopoli in the province of Bari, heiress to all. And she to-day is our companion and wife and co-worker in the great undertaking assigned us by Providence.

Having premitted these rapid notes that embody eighteen centuries of the history of this valley till to-day unknown and unexplored, and now become famous by reason of the prodigies here worked by the august Queen of Victories, let us now narrate more particularly the history of this blessed Sanctuary, where on the richest throne sits crowned,

. . . . *The fairest gem*
That shines in Heaven's high court.

§ 4.

THE VALLEY CHOSEN BY MARY AS CENTRE
OF HER GRACES.

Thus the modern *Valle* has for its centre the
Parish of the Most Holy Saviour in Valle and
the above mentioned Tavern of Valle. It is,
we repeat, on this small plot of ground that
the extraordinary events unfold themselves;
we therefore desire to call the attention of the
reader to it.

It is a hard task to try and describe the
abandonment in which the poor inhabitants
of this valley lived not more than fifteen years
ago; yet we will try to do it.

May we be allowed to quote certain particular incidents which here recur to our memory and which will serve to demonstrate
what a miserable state of existence these poor
country folk led.

We knew in 1874 a poor old man, whose age
unfitting him for work, sheltered his feeble
body at night in some oven, [1]) or else in some

---

[1]) In the Valle di Pompei every court, where grain
is beaten, has its oven, where the *contadini* bake their
coarse corn bread.

manger that by good fortune he might stumble
on. And in order to warm his poor members
chilled by the cold night air he would lie down
on some stable manure. At last one night he
sought refuge in a hayloft, which, no one knows
how, took fire, and the poor old man was
found thé next day burned by the flames, in a
pile of smoking hay. No one sought for any
information regarding him; moreover there
were no Carabineers in Pompei in those days.

And again, we visited a poor old woman of
Pompei, nearly eighty years old, and we found
her lying forsaken on an old bed, without
the assistance of any relative, as all were obliged to dig and till in order to live themselves
and nourish their beasts. On the wall against
which her bed stood, no image was to be seen,
not even that of the Friend and consoler of
the afflicted, the Crucifix. Ofttimes in carrying
her some strengthening food, we studied hard
to comfort her, but generally we could not
succeed in understanding her strangely draw-
led words, nor she ours because pronounced
in a manuer unknown to her. And so the poor
creature slowly neared her sepulchre, till one
day we found her dead, and she was no sooner
extinct than forgotten.

Moreover many families passed their lives
in the same hut, where the cow, the ass and
the pig were huddled together, all lying on
the same dirty straw, and father and mother,
sons and daughters all sleeping promiscuously.
Neither did there arise in their minds any
idea of having recourse to some authority or
to some charitable institution, as they had not
the slightest conception of what an authority
was, and much less still of public benevolent
societes belonging to the Commune.

But to which Commune and to which Society
could they have had recourse? As this Valley
was and still is dismembered into so many
Communes and Provinces that every year the
poor *contadini* in changing house or land,
change commune and province, mayor and
judge and tribunals? Oh why are these unfortunate ones of earth left so forsaken?

After a long study of these facts, it appears
to us that we have found the real reason of
such abandonment.

The reason lies in the irregular territorial
circumscription. Because this small spot of
Valle belongs to three different Municipalaties;
to Scafati, to Torre Annunziata and to Boscoreale; it also belongs to three provinces; that

is to say, under civil jurisdiction, to those of
Naples and Salerno, and as to ecclesiastical
jurisdiction it is under Nola, which is in the
province of Caserta. Hence being the extreme
limit of three communes and of three provinces
a certain forgetfulness on the part of both
communes and provinces was inevitable.

Even to-day great inconveniences arise because of such irregular subdivision, so that
the poor inhabitants have to suffer all the
brunt of them. Thus, merely to mention a
case, not only the waters of the river Sarno
that serve for the irrigation of the farms, but
all the overflow of the rain-waters and of the
mud that comes down from Vesuvius and Boscoreale passes through the middle of the com-
munal highway, as though we were living
in adamitic times. And this highway, the thoroughfare along which the products of this
Valley have to pass in order to reach Castellammare, belongs to three different Communes,
Scafati, Boscoreale and Torre Annunziata.

Hence it often happens that the road, rendered impraticable because of the overflow
of the waters, abounds in ditches so that the
carts and their contents are thoroughly shaken
up, and often overturned with a constant risk

5

to the life and health of these poor folk; and ofttimes the Most Holy Viaticum cannot be given to the dying as the road must be forded like a river.

Beside which law and civil justice and the Public Security suffer indefinable obstacles in their actuation. The poor contadini if they change the lease of a farm, and remove to a distance of but a yard or two, do not know to which Receiver to which Judge or to which Public Office to turn for the making out of contracts, citations and foreclosures; because within the distance of a yard they change municipality and province. So it is that yesterday for some suit, lease or foreclosure, they had to turn to the Pretore of Torre Annunziata, to the Tribunal of Naples and the Receiver of Torre Annunziata; to-day that they have rented a little dwelling opposite or next to their old one, they must have recourse to the Tribunal of Salerno, the Pretura of Angri and the Municipality of Scafati.

Thus for all lawless acts, contraventions and thefts that may occur along the public road, in the railroad station, and in the Square of the Sanctuary, the Carabineers of Pompei, who are nearest to the station of Valle di

Pompei, to the Workingmen's Homes and to the Via Sacra, and to the Hotel of the Sun, cannot interfere. For any act of authority recourse must be had to the Procurator of the King at Salerno, to the Pretura of Angri and to the carabineers of Scafati, but as all these places are rather distant from the centre of this valley, these latter are scarcely ever seen here; and even if they do appear they cannot exert their vigilance either over the Sanctuary, or the Asylums, or the Orphanage; over the bookbinding or tipography shop or over the houses of those who come to spend the summer in their villas, because all of these edifices are to the right of the provincial road, which belongs to the Province of Naples.

But this is not all. When the inhabitants of this Valley wish to marry, or are in need of a certificate of poverty or of any ecclesiastical document, they must turn to a third province, in Terra di Lavoro, to Nola. And how often cannot they do this; a few years ago many citizens to avoid the long journey and the expense entailed by the documents required of the Civil Bureau for their marriage, merely went to their Parish to perform the religious cerimony, without at all caring for all the future civil consequences.

Again, we were witnesses to the arrest, made by the carabineers, of a young man of twenty, accused of being refractory to the *leva* [1]); whereas he was not at all refractory; he had never been inscribed in the lists of birth in the Civil Bureau, because his parents, two old lessees of ours, had never contracted a civil marriage.

No later than 1888 a young girl about to marry, could find no trace of herself among the Acts of the Civil Bureau.

For which motive the Pretore of Angri found himself obliged to name a commission that would attend to the civil marriage of all the inhabitants of this valley, who had merely been married before the Pastor; and in order to enable them to do this, he was constrained to indemnify them for all expenses thereby entailed.

We now believe that we have given sufficient reasons to show the real motive why this unhappy population is so uniformily

---

[1]) The leva is the annual enrollment of all·youths subject to military service.

cheerless. But we trust that the blessed Virgin
will soon soften all their trials.

§ 5.

THE WITCHES IN THE VALLEY

And what religious faith had these almost
nomad inhabitants of the modern Valley?

The most abject superstition was commin-
gled with any religious belief they possessed;
prejudices and false ideas took the place of
the gospel truths. Without any hesitation
they had recourse to all sorts and manners of
witch craft, and they implicitly believed in all
witches and magicians.

One day (in 1878) I myself wished to see a
young calf that we were growing on one of
our farms.

— I wish to see your calf! — said I to our
farmer.

He looked around, and then in an irreso-
lute tone of voice, stammering his words, he
replied:

— Sir, I cannot lead it out of the stable. —

— And why so? —

— Because of the evil eye!... Supposing I
lead it out and the other farmers see it, and

exclaim — What a fine animal, — why I would be ruined. —

— Come, come, — rejoined I smiling — let me see it. —

— Then I must first exorcise all evil influences. —

So saying he took a handfull of earth, and threw some first on the animal's back and then on its neck, next he took the ring of the spindle of his old Mother, and the bone ring of his nursing babies, and placed them on the beast's horns. And so, having taken these superstitious precautions I was allowed to see the calf.

If anyone was suffering from some pain, or broke an arm, the relatives or friends would immediately call in a « *medicine-woman* » who would make a few signs of the cross on the arm or body, while muttering mysterious words; and they were firmly convinced that without the words of the pithoness, no pains ceased and no infirmities could be healed.

Of doctors and medicines there was no need. No sooner did some serious malady manifest itself than they would call the Pastor, he who was the first Pastor of the newly reinstated Parish, and who for all ills had one general,

common and infallible panacea, namely four,
eight or twelve bloodsuckers, till either the
sickness or the sick had to succomb of a
necessity.

Small ills were cured by going on foot to
Torre Annunziata, and there by the seashore
taking a good draught of salt-water.

Did anyone desire to take vengeance on an
enemy for some grievance, then they would
go to Cava dei Tirreni to find a woman who
made a public profession of witchcraft; five
francs placed in her hand, and the enemy was
bewitched.

— Sir — one day said to me one of our chief
lessees, who is still living, — I was once ill
unto death with a most mysterious pain in
my head. Well it was the witchery of another
farmer who wished to take my place in the
lease of the land I was then holding. And he
succeeded in his intent; little by little my life
began to wane. But having gone to Cava dei
Tirreni, and having paid the hag five francs,
she assured me, that while flying through the
air she had found the cause of the witchery,
and she consigned it to me; it was a ball stuck
full of pins. Now you will readily understand
that this same ball was meant to represent

my head and the pins the acute pains that
tortured me!

It was believed that when little children
remained puny it was due to witchcraft: and
when any theft occured they had recourse to
witches to find out the thief.

And it is believed by them to this day that
whosoever is born on Christmas Night will
assuredly become a witch or a *licantropus.* [1])

I do not speak of other facts in order not
to appear to exagerate, and I keep to the saying
of the Poet:

Ever to such truths as falsehood's mask do wear
Should lips of men be sealed and mute,
As shame, where least deserved, thus oft results.

§ 6.

THE VALLEY AND THE BRIGANDS.

To increase all this squallor there came at
last the period of brigandage.

---

[1]) See *Statistics of the Municipality of Scafati, presented*
to the Prefecture of Salerno, Anno II, 1863, page 50.

The memory of a certain band, headed by the famed Pilone, [1] that dreaded brigand, is still fresh in men's minds. This band, as far back as 1862, infested all the land lying round about Pompei, driving away not only the landed proprietors, but even such travellers as were obliged to pass through that part of the country; and those who did pass, because of sheer necessity, did so in the greatest fear and trembling. [2]

Add to this, what was worse than bringandage itself, a perfect infestation of petty thieves and highwaymen, who kept themselves in hiding in the recesses of the Amphitheatre and in a spot called *Lapillo*, where there were many ditches, resulting from the removal of

---

[1] See in the Journal «THE ROSARY AND NEW POMPEI,» February 1888, the fine description made by Count Ghirelli, Major in the 64th Infantry, Brigade Cuneo, then Commander of the forces that he had stationed in Pompei to repress brigandage.

[2] Pilone was so coragious and audacious that he ventured in full daylight to walk through the streets of Naples, and so it happened that one day coming down Via Foria, near the Botanical Garden, he was taken, after a sharp fight, and killed by some guards of Public Security.

lapillae, near the provincial road and not far distant from the Parish of Valle.

The sequestration of Marquis Avitabile, Director General of the Bank of Naples, and the spoliation of the governmental Procurator, assailed in full daylight, and the assassination of young Tortora, a teamster, whose name we will again refer to in the course of this history, are still clearly remembered.

Then came the period of the repression of brigandage and of the instantaneous shooting of any suspicious person, which served to heighten the dreadness of this valley; no one passed through here without terror, and those who saw it from a distance looked upon it as a place to be feared and avoided.

In the Annals of the Kingdom of Naples we find this note attached to the words Valle di Pompei: — a most dangerous resort of bold and infamous robbers. —

Thus the modern Valle di Pompei, solitary, sad, feared and avoided by all well intentioned and honest people well might have been called, as we have already termed it, the disconsolate Valley.

BOOK SECOND

The New Valle di Pompei.

CHAPTER I.

The First Day.

Such was the Valley of Pompei at the time our story begins.

To dream that a locomotive could come as far as this desert spot, to think of a post-office and a telegraph office, not to mention a busy railwaystation, would simply have been folly.

Whosoever had either said or even thought but fifteen years ago: This Valley within a short time will be the theatre of great portents in this our epoch; this Valley will be chosen by the Queen of Heaven to show her wondrous works to the XIX century; to this Valley after fifteen years people from all quarters of the globe will come to bend their knees before an altar here erected » — whosoever he might

have been that should have voiced these pre-
dictions wonld justly have been thought a fool.
And yet all this has come to pass.

How well I remember the day I first set foot on
this then melancholy plain; it was in the first
part of the month of October of the year 1872.

I had come hither to renew the leases of
the large farm belonging to the famous Tavern
of Valle, as my wife, Countess De Fusco, scarcely ever came to visit her lands. At that time
there was no detachment of carabineers stationed at Pompei, hence a traveller was in constant peril of sequestration.

As I arrived at the station of Pompei, I met
two of our farmers, armed with guns, who had
come to escort me.

It is sweet to me to-day, after so many remarkable events have taken place, to remember
how humble were the beginnings that gave rise
to all the great events that have transpired.
And tell me is it not a great delight to trace
out the origin of the works of God, and to look
over old memories, which often, beside being
a pleasure, are also of great benefit to the soul?

And so it is that I remember the first dialogue
that I had with those farmers, who had constituted themselves my safeguard.

While walking together along the provincial
highway toward the Tavern of Valle, at a certain point of the road, I turned to them with
an air of unconcern, and the dialogue which
ensued between us, carried on despite any
number of interruptions, as we found it very
difficult to understand each other; gave me in
the briefest possible time a clear insight into
the state and condition of things not only as
regarded the country but also its inhabitants.

— What new thing has occurred? Is it now
no longer safe to walk even along the provincial highway?

— Oh — spoke up one with a great air of
bravery — when you are accompanied by us
you have nothing to fear.

— What, are there any brigands about?

— Oh dear no, brigands indeed!... The band
broke up after the absence of Pilone.

— Absence? You mean death, — answered I.

— Pilone dead! answered the farmer, with
a sharp little whistle. — Pilone does not intend
to be found; they say he is dead; but instead
of that he is in hiding among the mountains
of Amalfi and of Agerola.

I looked at him in surprise, pitying the credulity of those poor people.

— But if Pilone has absented himself and is no longer here, what is the need of your going thus armed?

— Eh, eh — he answered with an ironical smile — there are robbers abroad.

— Robbers — continued I, slightly raising my eyebrows. — Robbers on the provincial highway? Where are the carabineers?

— There are no barracks here. And touching with his right hand the gun he carried over his left shoulder — We guard ourselves — he said.

So saying our little troop had happily reached a certain point near the Amphitheatre, where the two sides of the road form a rise, because cut through a mound of lapillae and ruins.

— Here we are at the *Pass of Valle* — said the other farmer — And here it is necessary to be very cautious, as robberies and assaults are perpetrated here without cease. — And here he began to count up all the persons he knew that had been assailed in broad daylight.

But when we neared the Tavern of Valle, and had already reached the old Parish of the Most Holy Saviour: — There — said he, pointing to a house lying a little behind the church, — it was there that one night the troops opened fire against some brigands who had taken refuge within. It was a truly infernal night; it poured and a furious wind was blowing. Oh, how much blood was shed.

This short account of a tragedy that had happened in our days, right near that old Amphitheatre, that recalled to my mind the streams of human blood that had there been shed in times of old for the pleasure of ferocious hearts, filled my spirit with sadness and drew a veil of melancholy over the pleasant and serene joys I had felt when I got out at the station of Pompei.

———

CHAPTER II.

The Solitary Church.

We had arrived at our destination. The first honors of our reception were paid us by the father of all these countryfolk, by the Pastor, a wiry old gentleman, with a fresh, rubicond face, and a gown and short cape that had braved many storms.

This kind Pastor was the first person with whom I was able to exchange a word in any intelligible kind of a language, as the inhabitants of the valley speak a very broad neapolitan dialect, and I with a closed accent, as we all of Lecce do, which made it a difficult matter either for me to understand or be understood. From him I first learned the name of this valley, which was called Valle a Pompeja, as he had concluded it must be because of all the facts we have already stated. With him we went to visit his parrochial church.

What a sight! That poor little church, built with the price of a sold bell, because the inhabitants had reached the number of fifteen, was so poor and small, so badly kept, that

Monsignor Formisano, the zealous Bishop of
Nola, at the beginning of his episcopal rule,
obliged the Pastor to sell a part of the fields
belonging to the Parish, in order to lengthen
it. And yet nevertheless it still remained too
narrow and small and was insufficient to
accomodate the population that daily kept
increasing; and whereas in 1840 the whole
modern Valle numbered scarce 300 souls, after
thirty years the number had increased to near
1200. And the church when crowded could
scarce hold a hundred people.

Beside which there was no sacristy, or sexton
to keep the House of God clean; nor was there
even a little room for the Pastor, who resided
on a farm of his nearly three miles distant
from the church. And as it had been badly
built and badly kept, the ceiling had cracked
and threatened to fall; for this reason it was
in 1880 pulled down by order of Cav. Ciro
Ilardi, at that time Mayor of Torre Annunziata.

There was but one Altar in the church and
that the High Altar, which was indispensable
for the conservation of the Most Holy Sacrament, but it was composed of old boards. And
it ought not therefore to surprise anyone when

6

I say that it was the peaceful abode of rats, lizards and bugs. — The inhabitants of this spot, save a very few families, are all field labourers and for the most part very poor —, thus wrote te Parish Priest to the Episcopal See at Nola.

Add to all this the fact that there were no schools to banish te darkness from these simple intellects; there was no temple in which they could all congregate and be instructed in the salutary principles of our religion; not even a single altar consecrated to Mary, to the Mother of God, the Consoler of the afflicted, around which they could gather and find comfort beneath the shadow of her celestial and maternal mantle. It is true that Monsignor Joseph Formisano, moved by his paternal zeal, had for many years been trying to build a church there; but he could not accomplish this design alone, overburdened as he was with the charge of more than 700 churches, among which were 85 parishes, exceedingly poor for the most part and some in construction. He had already lent a helping hand to the best of his abililties to many churches in his vast diocese that numbers more than two-hundred thousand souls, scattered among valleys and hills in four different provinces; and so he waited for Heaven to answer his ardent prayers.

Such was the state of and such the miserable worship in, the only church then existing here.

But hard as the zealous Bishop tried to make provision for so many needs, he could not obviate the fact, that many and many in this valley, because of the smallness of the church, could not assist at Mass on Sunday; and so the most part of this people not being able to enter the House of God, or hear His word, lived in perfect ignorance of the principles of religion.

But what saddened us most of all was to see on Sundays and other religious holidays the complete and public inobservance of the law of God as given in the third precept of the decalogue; to see young men and girls either work by the hour as on other days, or else pass the time in idleness, father of all vices; to see children, the most jealous part of the human family, from which some day will spring either the honest citizen or the thief, left to themselves, to grow up like brutes.

But how came this Image of Our Lady of the Rosary, that to-day astonishes the whole world with its portents, to be here in Pompei? How came this Temple, so grand and magnificent to rise here? And why and how came I, a total stranger to these parts, to be in the midst of so many extraordinary events arranged by Providence?

This is what I will frankly and simply state, hoping thus to benefit my neighbors.

———

CHAPTER III.

The Answer.

Reader, have you ever had your heart and mind enveloped by a cloud of sad, black musings, that have given you a feeling of irksomeness, of desolation and of being downcast?

You alone then can understand me.

Having scarce emerged from the dark forest of errors in which, as a follower of magnetism and spiritualism I had lost myself, my soul could find no peace. At the age of thirty-three, incessant, hard and implacable battles with Satan, who was constantly conjuring up new tempests with which to assail me, had beaten me down and obliged me to bite that dust, from which my proud head was wont to rise rebelliously and arrogantly against God. And here it was that God awaited me, that where iniquity had abounded there might grace and mercy superabound; it was one abyss calling another abyss. God is patient and longsuffering, because He is strong: being omnipotent He neither is angered nor takes vengeance, because all is subservient to Him. He is loving and gentle, of His own Nature good, that is to say lavish of His gifts, but just in punishing, because of our sins. He awaits man's penitence, but if he be obstinate, must, in justice, condemn him.

Oh great and merciful God! What if not Thy essential Bounty moved Thee to wait so long for my return to Thee, despite my distant wanderings, what if not the fact that all Thy ways are ways of mercy and of truth? Thou to my rebellions didst oppose Thine infinite patience; with the most gentle benignity didst Thow meet my wanderings; and when I offended Thee Thou answeredst with the sighs of Thy loving, generous, and paternal Heart. At last, after my repeated falls Thou didst stretch out Thy helping hand. Thou sawest my humiliation and my trials and sufferings, and then Thy mercy triumphed; for in the valley of humiliation Thou raisest the mountains of Thy grace. And the first fruit of Thy grace was to inspire me with an ardent, insatiable, uncontrollable desire of Thee, truth, light, food and peace of man, Thy creature. So it is my soul was anxiously seeking God. God alone, as the unique centre, could fix my intellect, floating in a fluctuating sea of errors. God alone could satiate the restless desires of a heart torn by numberless and burning passions.

One day, it was the ninth of October 1872, the tempest in my soul was torturing my heart and body more than usual, and filled me with a sadness not far removed from desperation. I went out of the house, a villa of the De Fusco's, and began to walk with a hurried and nervous step through the valley without well knowing where I was going. So walking I came to the most bleak and desolate part of this country, a spot the peasants call Arpaja, almost as though it were the dwelling place of Harpies.

All Nature lay wrapt in the deepest silence. I looked around me; not even the shadow of a living soul. Suddenly I came to a dead stop; my heart was bursting within me. In such darkness of being it seemed to me as though a friendly voice were whispering to me those same words that I had read, and that a true and holy friend of mine, now gone to his rest, was wont to repeat to me: « If you seek to be saved promulgate the Rosary. This is dear Mary's own promise. »

Who promulgates the Rosary is safe! This thought was like the lightning that flashes through the clouds on a dark and stormy night. Satan, who had held me as his prey, saw his defeat drawing near, and in a last desperate effort wound his coils more closely around me. It was the last battle, but a most terrible one.

With the audacity born of despair I raised my brow and my hands toward Heaven, and addressing myself to the sweet Mother-Maid: « If it is true » — I cried out, « that Thou didst promise to Saint Domenic that whosoever should promulgate Thy Rosary should be saved, then I will be saved, for I shall not leave this valley without having propagated Thy Rosary. »

No voice answered me; silence as of the grave encompassed me around. But suddenly a great calm succeeded to the dreadful tempest in my soul, and I felt that perhaps some day my cry of anguish would be answered.

The distant sound of a church-bell struck my ear and startled me; it was the noonday Angelus. I sank on my knees and voiced the prayer that a world of faithful addresses to Mary at that hour.

When I arose I felt that a tear had wet my cheek. Heaven did not make me wait long for an answer. The pages before you, reader, will soon explain all to you. Read and judge.

CHAPTER IV.

The first attempt.

And so I resolutely determined with all my
powers to promote the devotion to the Rosary
in this desolate valley, where by a strange
disposition of Providence I found myself, at
the time. But how was I to do it? How was
I to teach the Rosary to a people that lived
scattered in farms and cottages, without even
a site in which to gather them together on
a Sunday?

There was no other way than to go from
house to house freely distributing rosaries
and medals. As they were given gratuitously
they were gladly accepted, indeed by many
with a certain avidity, as being of metal they
appeared to those poorfolk to be of some value.

But what was the use afterall, when many
scarce knew how to recite the angelic salutation, the sweet « Hail Mary »?

But in coming into closer contact with this
people I noticed that they had an innate piety
and a profound reverence for the dead.

It was a great trial to them to see the bodies of their beloved being carried like carcasses to their last resting-place, without the accompaniment of some pious congregation, as they had seen in the neighboring towns, to recite the last prayers for the departed souls; it pained them to have no anniversary to perpetuate the memory of their ancestors in the minds of their descendants.

It appeared to me that I might derive some advantage from this feeling.

— Here — thought I to myself — is the instinct of the immortality of the soul. Their reverence for the dead, the undying memory they wish to keep of them, their prayers and suffrages are clear proofs that way down in the soul of man, no matter how ignorant, God has implanted the dogma of the immortality of the soul.

I took hope, and felt that this people, dispersed to the right and left, could more easily be led to congregate, when the object proposed was to their liking.

I therefore decided, in order to obtain my end, that my first step toward captivating their good will should be the establishment of a confraternity, whose duty it would be to accompany the deceased and to suffragate their souls by means of the recital of the Rosary. But there was this eternal obstacle where to have the confraternity congregate.

It was a heavenly day toward the end of October, a day that invited you to go out; and I, having no one with whom to converse, went out to hunt.

Beneath those long rows of poplars that line the banks of the river Sarno in the direction of the Royal Powder-Magazine of Scafati, I met a young huntsman; he was tall, wore gold eyeglasses, and was very affable. I was exceedingly glad when I learned from him that he was a priest. He was a native of the Valley and his name was Gennaro Federico. And continuing along our road I opened my heart to him about my wishes to form a Society of the Rosary among the « contadini, » so that they might fraternize among themselves and learn to recite the rosary, and also lend medicines and assistance to the sick, give dowries to indigent girls and christian burial to the deceased.

— It will be very difficult — he answered — This people has lost faith in such things — Nevertheless I would not allow myself to

become discouraged; and I questioned him closely as to the habits and customs of the people;
and I learned much from him; among other
things their great fondness for popular feasts,
games and merry-go-rounds and other such
like amusements, but especially the attraction
that raffles had for them; all the women of
the country round about would rush to attend
in the hope of winning a gold ring or a pair
of earrings.

— There — thought I to myself — is my first
expedient; to open a great lottery and distri-
bute rosaries, medals, images and pictures of
the Virgin of the Rosary as prizes. Thus after
the course of a few years every individual will
have a rosary, and every house will be de-
corated with a Picture of the Virgin of the
Rosary.

I decided in my mind to institute the lottery
together with a feast in honor of the Virgin
of the Rosary the very next October. Thus
at least by means of the ecclesiastical rites, the
panegyric, the fireworks, the popular games
and clamorous raffles, not only would the festival remain impressed on their minds, but
also the word Rosary, and the title of Virgin
of the Rosary.

And so I determined that the *first feast in honor of the Rosary* in Valle di Pompei should be celebrated during the month of October of the following year 1873; and that I would prepare for it a year beforehand.

§ 1.

THE FIRST FEAST OF THE ROSARY
IN VALLE DI POMPEI IN 1873.

And so it came to pass.

On my return to Naples, I began asking some pious ladies of my acquaintance for medals, rosaries, scapulars and pictures of any Saint. And I obtained them from the Baroness of Castro di Rosa, from Madam Catherine Volpicelli, from the Duchess of Trajetto and from Madam Raphael Piria. Many others I bought myself and with this big bundle I returned in the October of 1873 to my *new land.*

But I added two other articles. I had noticed that the Crucifix was not to be seen save in a very few huts, as it was customary with those people to buy a crucifix only on the occasion of a marriage; outside of this there was not even a rough wooden cross to be

found hanging on any wall. I therefore purchased several hundred crucifixes to be hung
at the head of the bed, and what is more I
firmly decided that that feast was not to be
lost in vapor like the smoke of fireworks and
guncrackers.

A principal feature of the celebration was
to be a great lottery, every ticket to cost a
cent. The first five prizes were to be of neapolitan gold, that is to say very showy, but
of small value, a ring, a pair of earrings, a
brooch, etc; the remaining 800 prizes were to
consist in crucifixes, rosaries and pictures of
the Virgin of the Rosary.

I ordered fire-works, games and the band
of Pagani for the festival.

As to the sacred rites there was to be a
Mass sung by the Pastor of Valle, who was
then Don Giovanni Cirillo, now deceased, and
there was to be a fine discourse on the Rosary
by my friend and confessor, P. M. Radente,
whom I had purposely invited and at my
expense.

Having no appropriate picture to expose I
took down a lithograph of the Madonna of
the Rosary from where it was hanging at the
head of my bed, and which I had bought in

Naples and offered it to the public veneration,
and with these preparations I awaited the
dawning of the first Sunday in October.

But contradiction began on the very first
day that I wished to do honor to the Queen of
the Rosary. The torrential rain and a perfect
hurricane accompanied by tunder and lightning, not only prevented the people from flock-
ing to the little parochial church and the
band from coming to Valle di Pompei, but it
kept the Pastor, the invited priests, our friends
and ourselves imprisoned within the parish
walls, unable so much as to put our heads out
of doors because of the weather.

— This is a bad beginning — thought I somewhat embittered, to myself. — It would seem
as though the Virgin did not approve of my
doings.

But then this afterthought comforted me
— I have nought else to do on my part but to
propagate the rosary. We will see if the Virgin
on her part will keep her promise made to
Saint Domenic that whosoever propagates the
rosary shall be saved. —

But my discouragement increased when listening to the fine discourse held by my aben all
mentioned confessor I noticed to my s bought

7

that very little of what he said was understood by the people who were there gathered together, as they were only used to hearing their own dialect and their own Pastor.

So it seemed to me labor lost and money wasted.

§ 2.

THE SECOND FEAST OF THE ROSARY
IN VALLE DI POMPEI IN OCTOBER OF THE YEAR 1874.

In order to forestall any hindrance the weather might place in the way of next year's festival I decided to leave to every family, as a visible reminder of the feast a pretty rosary and a picture of the Virgin.

And the October of 1874 having duly been ushered in I prepared another large lottery.

It was customary in that part of the country, when an invitation was to be made to the people at large, to send out a crier, and this latter was always some woman, known for her strong and stentorian voice.

So eight days before the time set, I sent out his woman to proclaim throughout that part the country the coming feast of the Rosary head three whole days I myself went about from farm-house to farm-house asking for any offering of corn or cotton, to celebrate the festival of the Virgin of the Rosary. House by house I entered and invited their occupants to come to the Parish, and to enjoy in the middle of the provincial road the great spectacles offered for their amusement, not to mention a great lottery.

From the sale of the corn and cotton I intended to draw two advantages; the first was to increase the sum that I had decided to spend of my own money; and my second and most important object, in which I succeeded wonderfully, was to thus sollicit these country people to come to the celebration as being personally interested in it. The festival succeeded quite brilliantly so that the inhabitants immediately understood that I had paid nearly all the expenses from out my own pocket.

But neither did I have in that year a fit Image of the Virgin of the Rosary to expose to public veneration. For this second Feast of the Rosary in Valle di Pompei I had another lithograph of the Virgin placed in the little tumble-down parochial church, beneath a small canopy, and around this picture were engraven in small compartments the 15 Mysteries. I had bought

7

it in Naples from Altavilla the Stationer, and
I left it to the Pastor of the Church in memory
of the feast.

Meanwhile, in order not to make another
mistake, I thought this time that no one could
better preach to this people than their own
Pastor, whom they would be able to understand.

I therefore begged him to preach three sermons on the Rosary to the people, hoping that
the words of their own Pastor would bear far
more copious fruit than the preceeding year.

But even this time I failed in my intent; for
instead of taking for his theme the Rosary he
chose to preach about the Salve Regina.

Nevertheless, the festival, the clamorous
raffle, the fireworks, the bombs and guncrackers, the noise of the drum of the band, the
public games, the donkey and bag-races, [1]) all
appeared to greatly satisfy my new people,
who, similar to all other country folk, at first
showed a certain diffidence toward a stranger;
but after witnessing the feasts two years running, and realizing that I was spending my

---

1) A kind of race much affected in Italy; it consists
in men, dressed in bags, who run for a prize.

own money to their advantage, they all grew to love me and feel great confidence in me.

But the feast, the sermon and the lottery were but merely a torrent sweeping through the land without leaving the ground fertile. The Rosary had not been learned, much less understood.

I was discouraged, but not disheartened. My object was none other than the propagation of the Rosary: I did not expect the fruit of my labors here.

I scattered Beads and medals broadcast among the poor, and having acquired their confidence, I began seriously to debate with learned and experienced prelates, as to the wisest and best way to firmly establish the devotion to the Rosary, already begun under such favorable circumstances.

Nobody could suggest anything better than to found a confraternity, which should meet all the needs of this people. But how attain unto this? How gather into a holy society all these people scattered throughout the land? How induce them to cultivate mutual love and brotherhood, when they were living far apart and in constant diffidence of each other? After a long discussion, we reached, perhaps by divine inspiration, the following decision. We

determined to call to our aid a Mission, which
rousing the souls of this people by the me-
ditation of eternal truths, should awaken in
those uncouth hearts the sure hope of pardon
through a sincere attachment to Mary and
especially to her Rosary. .

One day that I had gotten out at the station
at Portici, I met a priest, who appeared to me
both learned and zealous. And on questioning
him I found him to be a Missionary of the
Sacred Hearts, of which institution the Venerable Henry of Secondigliano was founder,
and having found out this much I opened my
heart to him, and told him how for a long time
the Lord had given me an earnest desire to
have a Mission come to Pompei. That worthy
priest belonged to the family Genovese of Pagani; in fact he was the brother of that Filo-
mena Genovese, Franciscan and Dominican
Tertiary, who died in odor of sanctity. He
greatly encouraged me and proffered his services; and from that day forth we were linked
together in close friendship. So with my mind
fixed on that point, I began to study by what
means I could actuate my design, which for me
was then a very arduous question, ignorant
as I was of all ecclesiastical matters, and a

layman and stranger to those parts, neither knowing the Bishop of Nola, or the Cardinal of Naples, who was at that time Sisto Riario Sforza, or any Prelate of the neighboring Dioceses.

But my designs were for the time crossed by the envy of him

« Who first upon his Maker turned his back ».

———

CHAPTER V.

The Hour of Mercy.

Some time elapsed, during which I never abandoned my plans and my firm purpose to make another attempt towards their actuation, when I one day in the name of the Countess de Fusco turned to two pious ladies, Raffaela Piria and Catherine Volpicelli, who had in the meantime raised a little marble altar in the tumble-down parish church after demolishing the old one made of worm-eaten boards. At the same time I was encouraged in my ideas by the Rev. Louis Caruso, then vicesecretary of the clergy of Naples and to-day a canon in that city's cathedral; he, being a friend of the Bishop of Castellammare di Stabia, who was then Monsignor Pedagna, had recourse to him for the choice of some holy priest to be sent on a missionary visit to Pompei. And yet nevertheless three long years elapsed before three priests conld be obtained to come on a mission to this desolate spot; because, as I have already stated, being a layman and a stranger in these parts, I not only was

ignorant of the manner of solliciting a mission,
not knowing to whom to address myself, especially as I desired it for a private devotion of
my own, but I even ignored the name of the
Bishop of Nola and of all the Bishops of the
surrounding Dioceses.

But when the day for the execution of
God's purposes arrives, there exists no obstacle that can offer any opposition to the
divine will.

The month of October of the year 1875 came
around in due season. In order to increase the
devotion to the Virgin, honored by the title
dearest to Her, I brought with me from Naples
a small statuette of our Lady of the Rosary,
which I carried to Valle on my own arms, accompanied by that worthy neapolitan priest,
Don Carlo dei Baroni Pellegrino Schipani;
and I placed the figure beneath a canopy in
the old parish church.

The feast in honor of the Rosary succeeded
brilliantly, partly because of the games, fireworks and raffles, and partly because of a
solemn Mass and Vespers sung by the Pastor
and the priests of the surrounding country.
Meanwhile I myself went from house to hut,
to invite the countryfolk to the feast, and

to encourage them to form a holy confraternity of Mary.

Having thus ordered matters, my first care
was to clean up and put in order as much as
possible the miserable little church, so as to
give it a slightly more venerable aspect. I
painted it in various places so as to hide the
enormous stains produced by dampness and
cracks, and put some quicklime in all holes
and crevices, in order to destroy the peaceful
nests of rats, lizards, spiders and sundry other
animals.

In order to accomplish this, I summoned a
young man of Pompei, a certain Pasquale
Matrone, the son of our oldest lessee. To him
I gave ten pounds of yellow, twenty pounds of
red, earth, a quantity of lime, white lead and
black smoke, and with this enormous provision of colors, and with an immense white-
washer's brush, the old parochial church was
painted, every one can imagine how.

But already the hour of mercy for this people
had sounded. The Bishop of Nola, just as my
hopes were about dying out, to my great and
unexpected good-fortune, authorized three holy
priests to undertake the sacred mission. And
on the second day of November of the year 1875

I went myself to Castellammare di Stabia to
meet those three blessed ministers, whose
happy lot it was to be the first to spread the
light among that people, lying in utter darkness. Their names are not only engraven on
our hearts, but what is much better, on the
maternal heart of Mary.

They were: Canon Santarpia of Lettere, to-
day passed unto a better life, Canon Don Giuseppe Rossi of Castellammare di Stabia, and
the priest Don Michele Gentile, Apostolic
Missionary, of Gragnano, who later on became the zealous chaplain of the Sanctuary
and is to-day in charge of a Royal Chapel in
Tuscany.

We were happy and proud to offer them
hospitality in our dwelling, the ancient Tavern
of Valle, and to wait on them ourselves; and
they did not disdain to occupy one of the
rooms which had but recently been added to
the structure.

What a touching spectacle! Old and young,
men and women, not only of the valley but
from all the surrounding country, flocked to
listen to the word of God, and as they could
not all find room in the little church, they
crowded around the entrance, right out in

the middle of the provincial road, exposing themselves gladly to the variable November weather. In the evening, after the sermon, these fields, a short while ago so mute and solitary, resounded with the sweet salutation to Mary, while the inhabitants, returning in groups to their homes, scattered to the right and left, chanting the Rosary.

The result showed the power of the Rosary and the pleasure of our heavenly Queen. All reconciled themselves with God, and settled their quarrels; many old enmities disappeared, and nearly all asked to be made members of the Confraternity of Mary.

It was the 12th day of November 1875, when the venerable Bishop of Nola, Monsignor Don Giuseppe Formisano, came to Pompei to administer the rite of Confirmation at the close of the spiritual exercises. It was the first time that I had the pleasure and fortune of meeting that Prelate. And it was then I made known to him the great longing that had been burning in my heart for three years, which was to raise in this land of Pompei, at my own expense, an altar to the Mother of God, under the title of the Rosary, in order to keep alive in the hearts of this people a devotion so beautiful, so useful to the soul, so approved by the church and so blessed by Mary.

Having heard my desire, and having learned from the three above mentioned priests the pitiful condition of the people, the holy Bishop, his heart touched with indescribable pity, turning to us and to the Countess de Fusco, the tears really gathering in his eyes, pronounced these memorable words, which were the origin of the great work of God in this spot :

— I consider it my duty to raise a church which shall gather together for divine worship all these poor people ; and for many years I have been looking earnestly to find at least one person to help me as this is the most remote point of my Diocese. But now that you wish to raise an *Altar* in honor of the Rosary, I propose that we raise instead, not an Altar, but a Church. Seek to find subscribers for a halfpenny a month; and so you will collect a certain sum on your part, while I on mine subscribe a subsidy of 500 francs. —

This proposition made to me after three years of vain efforts, in which I had not succeeded in raising a simple altar or any kind of a brotherhood among this povertystricken

people, seemed to me so strange and so ex-
ceeding my capabilities, that I was at first
taken a-back. In fact I turned to Canon Don
Giuseppe Rossi, saying:

— I fear that this is an astute strategy of
the evil one, who in order to hinder our carrying out a merely good plan proposes an excellent one; and so with the pretext of building
a church, which would require dear knows
how many years, comes to hinder the institution of the Confraternity of the Rosary, which
is already well disposed and ordered. —

But that worthy minister of the Lord thus
answered me:

— The counsel of our superiors is the voice
of God. Your good will is acceptable unto
God, but carry out the instruction of your
superiors.

And once again the pious Bishop of Nola,
having returned to Valle di Pompei after two
days and while under our roof repeated his
holy counsel. It was the hour of ten on the
morning of the twelfth of November of the
year 1875. The Pastor of the Church of Nola,
approaching the window in the middle room,
which looked out upon the old parochial
church of the Most Holy Saviour, and pointing

to a field adjoining the Parish, exclaimed in a prophetic voice:

— That is the spot where a temple must be raised in Pompei.

That Bishop was truly a prophet. But not even he knew the bearing of his words. Fifteen years had elapsed and that Temple not yet completed had acquired universal fame, and received its solemn consecration at the hands of a Papal Delegate, the most Eminent Cardinal Monaco la Valletta. At the end of eighteen Years (1894) that church begun for poor farmers received the sanction of its universality and of its greater glory by being raised by Leo XIII to the dignity of a Pontifical Church, and declared a Sanctuary of the world, under the dominion of the See of Peter in perpetuo.

The Countess on her part refused the undertaking, offering as an excuse her sorrow for the recent death of a son and her family cares. But I, whose great object was to end the battle with Satan, without thinking of the consequences of the undertaking, turning to her, said:

— Promise your consent to the Bishop and I will act for us both. Place your signature at my disposal, put me in contact with your acquaintances, and the Virgin will look to the rest.

But the wise Prelate, the Man of God, well knowing what immense obstacles the world and the devil generally place in the way of all the Lord's works, especially when the erection of churches is concerned, turning to us, remarked:

— You wish to build a church? But are you disposed to be called thieves and brigands, to be dragged through the streets of Naples like malefactors? If so then you will carry out God's work, for God will bless all your efforts, all your intentions; otherwise you will fail.

These authoritative words of the Anointed of the Lord, of the Head of this Diocese, still sound in our hearts and minds and give us courage in the midst of contradictions, and he was wont to repeat them to us as oft as he came to Pompei. And truly, we behold the Work of Pompei triumph marvellously over all difficulties, despite the hate of Hell, as it is the work of God and not of man. Yes, we frankly confess to it: we would never have had the presumption to begin the building of a great Sanctuary here in an open and desolate country, had it not been for the words of authority and comfort spoken by that holy Bishop, who e'en from the outset, as though he had been a prophet, prepared us to meet future trials; and had it not been for the still more powerful aid of Mary who upholds and strengthens us with her constant prodigies.

In this wise, spurred on by the Bishop's authority, I went to work. And making use of the name and influence of the Countess, I immediately wrote various letters to her many friends, generous neapolitan ladies, asking their subscriptions of a *cent a month*, so as to build a church to the living God on the land once given to the worship of false deities.

And so it is that the Lord, to show His power, sends down upon the poor human being, assailed by Satan, the rivers of His grace. *Suscitans de terra inopem et de stercore erigens pauperem.*

But it is now time to state how this Image of the Rosary, to-day become famous throughout the world for its miracles, was first found and brought to this desolate Valley of Pompei.

BOOK THIRD
The Miraculous Image.

CHAPTER I.

The First Entry into Pompei.

The three missionaries, and especially the
Rev. Father Michael Gentile, to whose share
it fell to preach the Rosary, had taught the
people to daily recite that form of prayer so
dear to the Virgin.

So it was that towards the end of the sacred
Mission I began to see my hopes realized, and
I rendered solemn thanks to God.

But in order to establish among this people
the habit of reciting the Rosary in common,
and thus to enable them to obtain all the indulgences granted to the Confraternity of the
Rosary, it seemed to me to be imperatively
necessary to expose to the public veneration
some picture of our Lady of the Rosary, at
whose feet the people might every evening
meet for the recital of their chaplet.

A picture of this description was not to be found here, save the small lithograph that I had given to the Pastor, as I have already stated. Moreover a picture to be exposed to public veneration, and that admitted of the gaining of indulgences, according to ecclesiastical liturgy, had of course to be an oil painting. To this add that I did not wish the Mission to close without my first having found and situated the devout Image, so that the three Missionaries might leave it behind them, as a reminder to the people to gather before it every evening and to recite their beads in common. This was the great object to which my desires tended.

It became therefore necessary for me to run to Naples and to find in all haste an oil painting of the Virgin of the Rosary.

And I went to Naples on the 14th day of November of that same memorable year 1875.

I began by asking myself and revolving in my mind whither to turn to find what I was looking for.

It occurred to me that ofttimes in passing along Via Toledo, near the Piazza Santo Spirito, my eye had rested on a shop-window in which various oil-paintings and pictures were exposed to the public gaze. And among others it seemed to me that I remembered one of the Virgin of the Rosary. I did not know the painter or his name even; but he was by surname, perhaps because a native of Foggia, called the Foggiano.

I therefore determined to direct my steps toward that shop. But a certain fear of finding myself very embarrassed overcame me, as I have never been able to bargain and squabble over prices as is the habit in Naples.

— Oh, I exclaimed if only I could take Father Radente with me. He, being a Neapolitan knows how to make such bargains. But where and how am I at this hour to find him?

I knew that ever since the Monks had been expelled from San Domenico Maggiore ten years before, he had lived together with two other Fathers, his companions, in a little house they had rented; and I was also aware of the fact that it was his custom to celebrate Mass every morning in the Church of the Rosary at Porta Medina.

— Very well — thought I — I will walk along Toledo; if it be God's will I shall find my friend otherwise I shall act for myself.

But Providence, Who with an invisible hand was directing and holding all the threads that were leading up to an event which in a short time was to be so wonderful, so disposed, that just as I reached the Square of the Holy Ghost, and very near the painter's studio, I met the venerable Monk.

This holy Friar was the man sent to me by God in the midst of my stormy life. On some other occasion, for the sake of gratitude, I will speak of him and of his virtues and tell how I met him and came to know him.

To-day I will limit myself to the statement that we first met each-other in this world's exile in the year 1865; and that we were divided here below in the year 1885; but it was in the intervening period, that is to say in 1875, that what I am about to narrate, took place.

The friendship with which Father Radente honored me, made me think of him as the right person to help me in the buying of a painting, having, as already stated, no correct notion of the value of such an object.

— Oh, Father, — I cried, no sooner had I espied him in the Square of the Holy Ghost — How fortunate I am to meet you.

And then and there I began to tell him everything that had taken place in those days at
Pompei; I told him about the visit of the Bishop of Nola, about the project of building a
Church, and of establishing a confraternity
of the Rosary, and finally I told him about
the picture I wanted to buy.

— The studio of the Foggiano is near here —
observed the Friar, — let us go there.

And together we entered.

In the front room of the shop there was a
canvass, representing the Virgin of the Rosary, but without the surrounding Mysteries,
and of such small dimensions as to scarcely
measure a metre.

— What is the cost of that painting?

— Four hundred francs.

— It is realy too much! — exclaimed Father
Radente.

I perhaps would have decided to buy it, but
the Father made me a sign and said:

— Come!

And when we were once more on the street
he said:

— Why spend four hundred francs on a
little painting, when you have now the intention of undertaking the expense of the

building of a church? Do you know what occurred to me while we were in that studio? Several years ago I gave to Sister Maria Concetta
De Litala, of the Conservatory of the Rosary
at Porta Medina, an old painting of the Rosary,
that I had bought in the second hand shop of
a merchant in the Via della Sapienza, and for
which I had paid three francs and forty centimes. Go and see it. If you like it, and if you
think you can make any use of it, old as it is,
ask it of her and she will certainly give it
you. At any rate it will suffice the country
folk of Pompei for the recital of their beads.

In the shortest possible time I reached the
Conservatory of Porta Medina.

— Please to call Sister Maria Concetta de
Litala — said I speaking through the grating
of the parlatory.

In a few moments I saw the sister, whom
I had known for a long time, enter the room.

— Father Radente has sent me to you, to
request you, if you are so inclined, to give
me that painting of the Rosary you have. I
must tell you that in Pompei the poor contadini
do not recite their orisons as they have not
an Image to arouse their devotion; and this
very evening I must carry them a painting,

so that the missionaries can show it to the people.

That fervent Tertiary, who really is a saintly woman, and who is still living, answered:

— I am only too happy that that poor abandoned picture should serve for such a noble purpose. I shall bring it you directly.

A few minutes later the sister redescended bearing the painting.

Alas! No sooner did my eyes fall on it than my heart stopped. Not only was the picture old and wormeaten, but the face of the Madonna, instead of being that of a Virgin all sweetness, holiness and grace, seemed rather that of some course, rough woman of the people.

— Who ever painted that picture? Mercy on us! — I could not prevent myself from exclaiming, with a tone of voice half way between fright and surprise. I felt in my heart that the poor Pompeians would find great difficulty in experiencing any sort of devotional influence and feeling any kind of love for the Rosary with such a picture before them.

To the deformity and unpleasantness of the face must be added the fact that a full palm of canvass was missing directly above the head. The mantle was cracked, and time and wormeaten, and in many places the colors had fallen off altogether because of the cracks. Nothing can be said of the hideousness of the other figures. Saint Domenic, on the right, more than a saint, looked like a street idiot; to the left was a Saint Rosa, with a fat, rough, vulgar face, who looked exactly like a country-girl crowned with roses. This latter saint, as I will relate further on, I had later changed into a Saint Catherine of Siena by the distinguished Comm. [1]) Federico Maldarelli, and as such she is to-day venerated.

Even the historical conceit in the painting was wrong, for the Queen of the Rosary was represented as seated, but without any diadem on her head, and instead of giving the chaplet of beads to Saint Domenic, as we are told she did in history, she was offering it to Saint Rose; and the Child Jesus on the contrary is the One who is giving the rosary to the spanish patriarch.

I hesitated whether to refuse it or whether, under the circumstances, to accept it. I was

---

1) Commendatore is an italian honorary title given to men who have greatly distinguished themselves by personal merit.

tormented by the idea that the Mission was
drawing to a close, and that I had uncondition-
ally promised a picture to the three missionaries and the people for that very evening.
And all knew I had come to Naples for the
purpose of buying a painting and were expecting me to bring it with me. What was I to do?

— Do not think too long about it! said the
Sister to me with a sweet accent of reproach.—
Take this picture with you, it will certainly
succeed in eliciting a Hail Mary.

Constrained by necessity, but much against
my will, I consented. But how take it with
me? Here was another drawback. Its size,
measuring as it did a metre in width and a
metre and forty centimetres in length, prevented my carrying it with me in the railroad-
coach; nor yet had I the time to have a box
made or to have it sent in any other way, as
I had promised to bring it with me.

— Oh do take it with you, — gently insisted
the good Sister. — What matters it if you do
stand up in the coach? Take the Madonna
with you!

But this proposition which implied my traveling fourth class, and so of course standing up
and holding the picture, did really not suit me.

At this juncture the Countess, my wife, arrived at the entrance, and the good sister, her face quite illumined, and with the accent of one inspired, said, turning to her;

— You must take this painting with you, and at this very moment!

And the Countess in order to gratify her, took the picture, had it wrapped in a sheet and thus having placed it in a carriage we took it to our home which was then in the Via Salvator Rosa, N. 290.

But the great question was to get it that evening to Valle di Pompei.

Suddenly while thinking the matter over, it occurred to me that the teamster of Pompei, by name Angelo Tortora (the only one who made trips between Naples and Valle di Pompei) was on that very day to return home with his load. His great business was to empty the stables of the wealthy families of Naples, and to sell the manure to the farmers in the country.

I sent for him to come to us.

At that hour Angelo Tortora had already filled his cart and was about starting on his way to Pompei. No sooner did he receive my embassy than he immediately came to our house.

— My friend — said I — you must please
do me the favor to take this picture to the
Parish Church of Valle this very day. As soon
as you reach there consign it on the spot to
one of the three Missionaries that you will
find there.

Angelo Tortora was the man who had a large
share in my labors during the first years. He
was one of the leading men among the farmers
of the Valley, and also one of the best off in
this world's goods.

Very tall and with exceedingly robust mu-
scles and square shoulders, he had a loud and
sonorous voice and always talked in such a
tone as though he were speaking to the deaf.

I had often made use of his services on my
various tours through the country when in
search of corn and cotton for my feasts of the
Rosary and the noisy raffles. It was he, who
mounted on a bench in the middle of the pro-,
vincial road, directly opposite the Parish, and
under the shadow of the De Fusco dwelling
(the ancient Tavern) called out with his sonorous and stentorean voice the numbers of
the Lottery; and from this rustic stage he
called by name each of the winners of the
rings, rosaries and pictures, each and all of

whom he distinguished in the midst of an immense crowd.

So this was the man for me, and I had no need of repeating my request.

— All right — he answered, took the picture and went away.

And so while the Image was wending its way along the provincial road toward Pompei on Angelo Tortora's cart, I ran to the station to catch the train and precede its arrival.

But what was our displeasure when having reached Valle di Pompei in the evening, we learned that Tortora had brought the painting *by actually laying it on the top of the manure* with which his cart was already laden. He, desirous of helping me, had not known how to do better. But when I called for him to pay him for the transport, he refused, saying it *was enough for him to have carried the Picture of the Madonna.*

Poor man! He never knew that his name would appear in this History, which will last as long as the Sanctuary of the Virgin of Pompei. Let us hope that the Virgin will now remunerate him in heaven for all he did on earth for her Temple.

Now who would ever have believed that that old canvass, bought for three francs, and which entered Pompei on a dung-cart, was in the designs of Providence ordained to become the means unto salvation of innumerable souls? and was to become so precious as to be covered with the most refulgent diamonds and rare gems? and was after a short interval to be raised to the richest throne in a monumental Temple, expressly built for it? and that it would have called to its feet not only the poor country-folk of Pompei for the recital of their devotions, but a crowd of worshipers and pilgrims from strange lands, thus becoming at the same time a centre of religion, of civilization and of glory; and that it would have attracted the attention and the love of the High Head of Christianity to such an extent as to have Him place the Sanctuary of Pompei beneath the aegis of His Papal Mantle?

Oh, had we been able to predict and foresee it! — Had all of those, who to day are the beloved children of the Queen of Pompei known it, and who come, from Malta and Madrid, from Liverpool and Coblenz, from Brussels and Warsaw, from Vienna and Blois, from Switzerland, from Africa, from China and

from the Americas, not to mention our own
Italy, second to none in doing Her honor, to
present unto her, together with their supplications, the offering of their gratitude! Oh had
we been able to divine that sublime secret!
We would have rushed to remove her from
that dirt-pile and we would have carried her
on our arms, we would have had Her brought to
this abandoned spot beneath a rain of flowers
and amidst the hosannas of a thousand voices
exclaiming: — *Blessed is she who is sent unto
us by the mercy of the Lord.*

CHAPTER II.

The First Restoration.

Tortora having reached Pompei with his
load had immediately consigned the painting,
so ardently expected, to one of the three missionaries in the little tumbledown parochial
church. But when that Image was disclosed
to the gaze of the people there present, among
whom we remember the already mentioned
three missionaries, the old Pastor in person,
the Priests Gennaro and Romualdo Federico,
brothers, and the family of the Countess De
Fusco, and several others, no one could prevent a certain smile from wreathing around
his lips at the sight of that daub which I
had brought to expose to public veneration. All
agreed that in its actual condition the picture
could not possibly be placed in the church.

And so for that evening of the 14th of November I had to be satisfied to see the fruit
of my trips placed in a corner behind the
Altar of the Parish.

On the following day we all met in the church
to take counsel. It was absolutely necessary
for the painting to be restored. There was not

sufficient time to send it back to Naples to have
it retouched, neither did the old daub seem to
warrant the expenditure of even a cent on it.

—I know an old painter—(broke in Don Gio-
vanni Cirillo, the old Pastor) who paints views
of Pompei, and works within the walls of the
Amphitheatre, a certain Mr. William Galella.
He is a good christian and a penitent of mine.
Perhaps he would charge you nothing, or at
least very little, when he hears of the matter.
Let us send for him.

Shortly after the painter Galella, who is still
living, arrived. He, having seen the picture,
asked for time to retouch it, as it required the
adding of bits of color and of varnish; which
had fallen off the canvass.

— This painting was given us as a present —
I repeated to him — in order to introduce among
these poor toilers of the soil the devotion of the
Rosary. Hence there is neither Confraternity,
nor parish, that can stand the expense of having
it restored. However I will gladly spend a small
sum myself. Mind, this picture only cost three
francs, forty centimes, but I will give you
twelve francs, seventy-five centimes if you
will render it fit to be exposed in church.

And he took the painting.

The Mission was at an end. The three good priests had returned to their respective homes rejoiced beyond measure at having gathered in such an abundant harvest unto the Lord.

A week, two weeks, three weeks pass and still no picture.

Fortunately these country-people, having become docile to the voice of the missionaries, continued to meet every evening in the old Parish Church to recite the Rosary before the little engraving which I had exposed in the famous feast of 1874. I however did not wish to let the occasion escape me of founding the much desired Confraternity of the Rosary, so that no sooner should the Image arrive, than each member could immediately begin to enjoy the indulgences.

In order that a Confraternity of the Rosary may enjoy all the indulgences and privileges granted by the Supreme Pontiffs to the Dominican Order, it is necessary that the General of the Order should send a Diploma of Foundation, naming a Director and that the diocesian Bishop should approve both the one and the other.

9

Now I myself, who because of the great love
I bore Saint Domenic was already aggregated
to his Third Order of Penitence, and never
allowed any occasion to pass to induce others
to love and venerate the white vestment of the
holy spanish Patriarch, would have desired
with all my heart that my friend, Padre Radente, might have been nominated Director
of the new Confraternity.

And having returned to Naples I opened my
heart to him on the subject.

—I cannot accept—answered Father Radente
with his usual gentleness — because though
the Convents are disbanded I still live in community with other Fathers in Naples and I
belong to the Diocese of Naples, and I do not
wish to lose my sonship of the Convent of
San Domenico Maggiore. Hence I cannot at
the same time be the Director of a Confraternity in Pompei, that is under the authority of
another bishop, and live in community with
other fathers in another Diocese. It will be a
great deal if you can obtain from the Bishop
of Nola a permission allowing me to come to
Pompei to confess you and the people. In this
case my coming, every time you shall call me,
will be profitable.

I had to be satisfied with this answer, and he himself wrote to Rome to his General asking for the Diploma for the foundation of the *Confraternity of the Most Holy Rosary in the Valley of Pompei,* and proposing as its Director the venerable priest, Don Gennaro Federico, a resident of those parts.

Nothing in this world happens by chance; but every thing, as our great Dante says « *is well disposed unto a foreseen end.*

The reader will already have recognized in that name the same young priest whom I had first met in Pompei beneath the long rows of poplars that line the banks of the Sarno. And the General Superior of the Order of Preachers, who was the Vicar General Father Giuseppe Maria Sanvito, lost no time in sending him the desired Diploma, bearing the date of the twelfth of December of that same year 1875.

The Diploma was sent to Nola to be signed by the Bishop, and with these waits the whole month of December passed.

CHAPTER III.

The year 1876.

§ 1.

THE MITE OF THE WIDOW IN THE GOSPEL.

Then came the month of January of the year 1876, of that year the memory of which will never be cancelled from the minds of men, for it opened the era of great mercies and wondrous miracles in this land, once the home of desolation and of death.

A bright sun shone in the clear and azure sky in the early morning hours of the first day of that memorable year. The balmy, windless, air, for in this Valley there is generally quite a strong breeze blowing, made the New-Year day seem more like Easter. This is not a rare occurrence in this part of the country, where the fire of Vesuvius and the vulcanic sand, that forms the understrata of the soil, change the rigid cold of winter into a mild and temperate atmosphere. A single ray of sun here is enough to change the frigidity of winter into the tepid warmth of spring.

The prudent Bishop of Nola had given us two good pieces of advice; the first was not to undertake any building till we had collected a sum sufficient enough to meet the first expenses; and the second was not to exceed for any-one the quota of the monthly offering which was to be *one penny.*

— Two cents a month — said he — after a year or two tire the giver; but one cent matters nothing to any-body.

He also suggested our seeking the sub-scriptions of the peasants, not only to exercise them in the christian duty of alms giving, but also to let them feel that they had a part in the building of the Church which was intended for their spiritual wellfare.

I therefore had to begin my peregrinations across the fields, but this time for a nobler purpose than before, not to institute a country feast but to help build the House of God. And so on that first day of the New Year together with the first friend I had met in Pompei, the priest Father Gennaro Federico, I began my journeyings from house to home to collect the peasant's mite.

How it rejoices my heart to day to reread in a little book I jealously preserve, the names of those poor field-laborers, whose offerings were the first fruits consecrated to our dear Mother.

The subscribers in Pompei numbered three hundred, and therefore the rich harvest of that year amounted to *fifteen francs*, three dollars.

And yet at that moment those fifteen francs did not appear to me a sum to be despised, nor an unworthy beginning. I remembered the widow's mite and the solemn words of our Lord, recorded in the gospel of St. Mark: — Verily, verily, I say unto you this poor widow has given more than all the rest. —

Those fifteen francs, heavy as the thousands of the wealthy, were the first seed that was soon to produce so rich a harvest.

The poor were the first to give their offerings to that humble church that was in so short a time to become a worldrenowned Sanctuary; and the poor of all countries have followed that example. And the mite of the poor, that mite that draws down such copious blessings from Heaven, has helped to increase the majesty and riches of this Temple sacred to God.

So it was decreed by an inscrutable Providence. In olden times they were kings and popes, princes and wealthy abbeys, who, backed by their riches, undertook the erection of sumptuous churches and the foundation of new social and religious institutions.

In Pompei the order of things is reversed. A Temple has risen that is monumental and that calls to its arms the people of all nations, but its foundation stone was bought with the fruit of the sweat of the brow of humble toilers of the soil; its increase will not be founded on any fixed income or capital, or on the subsidy of a government or of a municipality, nor on the help of a Prince of the Church or of the State, or on the protection of a magnate or an emperor. No; but it will be the fruit of the uncertain, eventual and spontaneous mite given by the charity of individuals. And its future?..... Oh it will rest secure and unshakable on the innumerable benefits conferred by the Mother of believers, on the tears dried by Her, on the sorrows She will have softened, on the sores into which she will have poured Her healing balm.

§ 2.

THE FIRST FRUITS OF THE CITY OF NAPLES.

I very clearly understood that with only the offerings of the peasant-folk of Pompei on which to start it would be simply impossible to build a church however small; and for this reason I built my hopes on the numerous acquaintances that the Countess De Fusco and I had in Naples.

The Countess first turned her steps toward the Largo Petrone alla Salute where a cultured and pious young neapolitan lady, Miss Catherine Volpicelli, had founded the Pious Working-Union of gentleladies intended to help along poor churches. And the lady upon whom the Virgin's choice fell for her first promoter was Mrs. Maria Irbicella, the wife of Mr. Domenico Irbicella.

At first she refused, or rather excused herself, saying she could not succeed well because of her numerous domestic occupations, having many children, and because of the great number of worthy charities recently instituted in Naples, and all dependent on private bounty,

and all founded on the same determined number of charitable people. But the Virgin whose
intent it was to make use in the erection of
her Sanctuary of such persons as the world
deemed the least fitted, so blessed her efforts
and good will that in a short time hundreds
of families, inspired by her zeal, subscribed
to the incipient work of a future church in
Pompei, which as yet was more in the desire
than in the fact. Then Madam Irbicella was
the centre toward which all the offerings
poured and she was the principal promulgator
in Naples; but not being able to collect all the
sums herself she chose other promulgators,
and the offering was always, as had been
decided, a penny a month.

It will be easy to understand that among the
first subscribers was the allready mentioned
Catherine Volpicelli not to speak of other
« promoters » of the Heart of Jesus. Among
these latter we will never forget two really
privileged and virginal souls, which now
follow the Lamb in Heaven whereever He leads.

The first of these was the Princess Mar-
gherita di Santobono, the Mother of the Third
Order of Saint Dominic in these our days, a
woman of eminent piety and heroic charity,

who loved Countess De Fusco and myself with
sisterly love. The other was the exemplary
young girl Ernestina Freda, whom the Madonna at an early hour chose as a helpmate
to the Countess; and for five years she was
the latter's indivisable companion in the difficult task of going from house to house asking
for the monthly subscription of *one penny*.

Ernestina Freda always bore with perfect
patience and in silence all the hard words and
cross faces, all the cold and bitter remarks,
which during the course of five long years, in
her visits to strangers, were directed against
the Countess De Fusco by persons who naturally could never believe that a church could
be erected with *a penny* a month, and that in
the midst of a desolate and abandoned country.

Ernestina Freda, though small in her person,
was the type of a strong, untiring woman, with
an iron and indomitable will; and with a body
crushed by continual infirmities, she conquered
her physical weakness to devote herself wholly
to the task of laboring for her Lord.

No sooner did I make the acquaintance of
that hard-working, christian, soul, than I hastened to present her to Father Radente; and
in a short time she became a most fervent

member of the Third Order of Saint Dominic, and she chose for her field of labor the poor church of the Dominican Fathers on the Vomero, and for its benefit she consumed the course of her christian apostleship.

The name of this noble Tertiary, who was a model of christian modesty and active charity in the midst of society, will not only remain written in the memories of the church of Saint Mary the Free on the Vomero, but also in the pages of the History of the Sanctuary of Pompei.

As to myself I strove to be equally fortunate. And the first house I visited was that of the Baroness of Castro De Rosa, who resided in the Montemiletto palace in Via Toledo. She subscribed not only for herself but for her whole family and also directed me to the excellent family Ricciardi that lived opposite. And when the pious widow Concetta Galluccio, now in Heaven, heard the great news that in the desert country round about Pompei the Banner of the Rosary was to be planted, she was so rejoiced that she hastened to speak of the matter to her numerous friends and relatives and to her brothers, Fathers in the Society of Jesus. Very soon the Pandolfelli family and all the party that were wont to gather together in their home in the evening for a conversation, subscribed their names.

I also sought out those two illustrious families that do honor to the neapolitan aristocracy, and who had a great friendship for me; I mean the family of the Marquis Francis Imperiali, a truly noble and beneficent type of man, and that of the gentle Marchioness of Latiano, Irene Imperiali, who induced her whole family to take a part in this holy undertaking.

§ 3.

THE IMAGE REBLESSED — THE INSTITUTION OF THE CONFRATERNITY OF THE ROSARY IN VALLE DI POMPEI.

January 1876 was drawing to a close. One day we were notified that Galella had come to consign us the painting; and such was really the case.

The poor painter had not been able to do better; to all the cracks and spots eaten by time and by woodworms he had applied some paint and stucco to hide the old wounds; and then he had neatly varnished over the whole picture so as to make it appear new. But the face of the Madonna was still the same, common and unpleasant to look on; the diadem over her brow was still lacking as likewise the space of canvass, absolutely necessary to produce an artistic effect, to prevent the head from touching the frame. Beside which Saint Rose was still the rubicond, fat peasant with the crown of roses, whose white dress without fold or shadowing looked exactly like a heavy board leaning against her chest and throwing her over with its weight.

But at least, thus restored, it could be presented to public veneration, without fear of its being interdicted by the Holy Visit.

Having received the picture with some satisfaction I turned to the painter with a pleasant manner and asked him his price.

— Sixty francs. —

— What! *Sixty francs!* The whole thing only cost *three* francs and you want *sixty* for a rennovation? —

— I have said sixty francs, and my trouble is worth a great deal more. What with varnish, gypsum and paint I have spent that sum. —

— If that is the case take the painting yourself and sell it for your own profit. I will again expose my engraving till the new Church is built. —

But the painter who really was a good christian, when he better understood the destination of the image and the interest that those poor peasants showed in the erection of their little church, not only no longer wanted the sixty francs, but of the thirteen I had offered him at the outset he would only accept ten and handing me the remaining three, said:

— I desire to be the first to help in the building of the new Temple. —

And in fact the three francs of the painter Galella were the first fruits of Art consecrated to the new Church of Pompei.

Oh! had the painter Galella only known that he was the first to head that long list of artists who by their spontaneous work in this Sanctuary have immortalized their names in heaven and earth! He would have been much happier had he known that Providence had elected him to be the first man to put his hand to that Image which was soon to receive the veneration of so many divers peoples.

. .

February came.

The picture was at last ready, and the Diploma authorizing the erection of the Confraternity had returned from Nola with the Bishop's signature: nothing remained to be done but to have the Image reblessed, to canonically erect the Confraternity, and to destine an altar for the veneration of the Rosary, on which to expose the Image of the Virgin, and to which indulgences were attached. But even here there were new difficulties to meet.

In the small Parish there were but two Altars; one, the High Altar dedicated to the Most Holy Saviour where the most blessed Sacrament was kept, and which, as we have already told, had recently been rebuilt in marble at the expense of the above-mentioned Pious Union of ladies; the other had been raised by help of the contributions of the peasant-folk and dedicated to Saint Francis of Assisi.

After a long talk with the priests and with the old Pastor it was decided to ask the consent of the Bishop of Nola, to temporarily remove, till the first chapel of the new Sanctuary was built, the painting of Saint Francis, and substitute that of the Rosary.

The country-people were well satisfied, and, as is here customary, I notified them by a public crier — To all meet in the Parish on the second Sunday of February, the 13th day of the month, to found, as habitual, by voice of the people, the Company of the most Holy Rosary.

I chose that day purposely, as it is the feast-day of that great Tertiary of the Third Order of Saint-Dominic, Saint Catherine of Ricci; and I, as a Tertiary, chose every opportunity to try and induce others to love and desire my beloved Third Order of Penance.

The day fixed for the great event having arrived, all the people gathered together in the small Parish. I had obtained permission from the Bishop of Nola to have Father Radente himself, already invited by me come from Naples to rebless the rennovated painting. And while the crowd applauded he read the Diploma of the General of the Order, with which the Priest Don Gennaro Federico was nominated Director, and the *Society of the Most Holy Rosary in Valle di Pompei became a partaker in the indulgences, privileges and merits of the three Orders of Saint Dominic.*

After which he received into the third Order the Pastor and Father Federico and eleven other inhabitants of the Valley. So that on that day the Virgin rewarded my efforts, by granting me the greatest joy possible, which was to see founded here the Confraternity of the Rosary, so dear to Her, and at the same time to behold the beneficent branches of the Third Order of Saint Dominic, which is the School for Saints through which to ascend to Heaven, planted.

Oh how happy was that kind Director of my soul when on returning to Naples in the evening, he told the Dominican Fathers, his companions, how the *old picture he had bought for three francs had served to erect in Pompei the Confraternity of the Most Holy Rosary.*

Thus humbly began that Confraternity of the Rosary of Pompei, which in a few years has spread its peaceful ramifications not only throughout Italy, but over all the parts of the world, so as to comprise more than two million members, among which figure Bishops and Cardinals, Princes and Queens, and the greatest name of this century, the Representative of Christ, Leo XIII.

———

CHAPTER IV.

The second Rennovation of the Picture of the Virgin.

But in order to complete the history of the painting so venerated to-day, it is well that I should here bunch the events that occurred four years after that festal day.

Commendatore Federico Maldarelli, a well-known neapolitan painter, three and a half years later, that is to say in May 1879, seeing the daily increase in the veneration so many neapolitans and strangers felt for the Virgin of Pompei, moved by his great piety, offered to gratuitously and much more completely rennovate the painting, which, because of the extreme dampness of the Parish Church, had almost completely deteriorated, and put a certain design of mine to effect, which was to have the Saint Rose changed into a Saint Catherine of Siena. Both of these Virgins of the Lord belonged to my Third Order of Penance; in fact the former of the two is the glory of the Americas, *the first saint* that the newly discovered and christianized world gave to the Church. But I preferred to behold kneeling near the Virgin of the Rosary in the new church my especial patroness, that Angel of Fontebranda, that Seraph of Siena, first because an italian and the glory of Italy and all Christianity and secondly because the Mother and most especial Mistress of this same Third Order.

I therefore requested Maldarelli to please change the crown of roses of Saint Rosa into a crown of thorns, the distinguishing sign of our italian virgin, and also to have two wounds appear in the palms of her hands to recall her venerable stigmata.

But there remained one arduous task, namely that face like a full moon, which if wholly unfitted for a Saint Rosa, was simply out of the question for a Saint Catherine, woman of a delicate constitution and gentle features, such as we see in the only portrait of her extant, painted by Vanni and preserved in the church of Saint Dominic in Siena.

The courteous neapolitan artist promised to do his best to satisfy me.

So the Countess De Fusco on the following day took the painting with her in her carriage from Pompei to Naples and left it in the book-store of Signor Salvatore Festa, asking him to see to it that the picture was conveyed to the celebrated painter's studio.

But already in the course of these three years the Queen of the Rosary had shown signs of her approval of and her pleasure in the growing work in this Valley, and the erection of a temple sacred to her, by many graces and prodigies. And many ladies and gentlemen had begun to undertake pilgrimages from Naples to this Valley to thank the blessed Mother for favors received or to ask for new ones.

So it did not seem just to me that persons should come to Pompei to render thanks to the Most Holy Virgin and should find no image to venerate. Moreover the popular devotion which so often takes to a certain painting, to some special sculpture, to some particular color, dress or form, beneath which it is wont to daily venerate the Madonna, ran the risk of cooling somewhat. What was to be done?

The bounty of God, which gives rise to and then completes the good will of man, did not even fail me this time, and helped me to find an expedient, which in its turn also produced other extraordinary events.

. .

My favorite resort in Naples at that time was the dear little church of the Rosary at Porta Medina.

It was thére that together with my lamented friend and spiritual adviser Father Radente and with Doctor Giuseppe Gaetani, we had, as far back as January 1874 gathered together a society of ladies and gentlemen, all belonging to the Third Order, and every month we were wont to hold there our pious meetings. And it was because of the devotion of Doctor Gaetani and myself to Saint Cecilia, that the *twenty-second* day of every month was irrevocably fixed upon for the sacred conference. And the same custom still holds to-day in the church of San Domenico Maggiore to which our Tertiaries moved in 1885.

The soul of this congregation of the Third Order in the church of the Rosary at Porta Medina was that same Tertiary who gave me the first picture of the Virgin, I mean Sister Maria Concetta De Litala.

To her therefore did I turn in my perplexity. And she told me that Father Radente at the

same time that several years before in Via
Anticaglia he had bought for three francs
fourty centimes the picture of the Virgin of
the Rosary, had also purchased another painting of the same size and by the same author,
representing the *Nuptials of Saint Catherine of Siena*. Now it is well to'know that
that venerable man, because of his great
love for the Rosary and for his patroness
Saint Catherine of Siena, thought he was following an impulse of piety, when seeing the
two objects of his heavenly love in the middle
of a street thrown down among old second-
hand ware and wretched pictures, he bought
them and carried them away, in order to remove them from such a humiliating position.

And the Sister also owned this second
picture given to her by the good Father.

— Very well — said I — you gave me the *first
picture* so as to plant the love for the Rosary
in the hearts of the peasants; and you will
also give me *the second,* so that the devotion
which has increased not only in their hearts
but also in those of the neapolitans, shall not
suffer diminution.

The Sister, rejoiced to find herself an instrument in the hands of God and thus enabled

to benefit distant souls, and to increase the devotion to the Rosary and to Saint Catherine, immediately brought me down the painting, which to tell the truth was as old as the first but not quite so hideous or woebegone.

It represented the Virgin of the Rosary with the Babe in her arms, in the act of giving the ring of the celestial nuptials to Saint Catherine. Saint Dominic it is true was missing, but there was a certain charm about the face of the Virgin; and the Saint of Siena was not as repellant as the Saint Rose in the other painting, so it appeared to me to have gained something.

The peasants, thought I, will not mind the substitution. After all it is the Virgin of the Rosary I am presenting to their veneration.

But a black, discouraging doubt arose in my mind:

— Will the favors continue to flow down from Heaven when I shall have changed the Image? —

— Oh, without doubt — answered I to myself. — It is not the Image that works miracles in Pompei, but it is the power of God clearly manifesting itself there, because He alone can do great and admirable things: *Qui facit mirabilia magna solus.* The Image is but the

simple instrument of His prodigies. But God
desires, and to-day more than ever, that the
most perfect creature ever formed by His hands,
the divine Mother of Jesus, should be honored
in this world; and He wants her honored and
venerated by all peoples with one accent: *Ave,*
and with one same hymn, *the Rosary.* It is therefore the Rosary which draws such copious
benedictions from Heaven; it is the *Church
of the Rosary* the Virgin wishes to see built
in Pompei, as She shows by Her miracles.

I was not mistaken: my new undertaking
of thus changing or rather contrasting with
the habits of the people was crowned with
success. The second picture placed in the same
spot whence the first one had been removed,
received the same veneration; and new and miraculous graces poured down from Heaven on
the many who associated themselves to the new
work, or who came here to implore new favors.

The heavenly Virgin deigned to prove to me
by facts, that She showered Her blessings on
this abandoned land for the prediliction she
bears her celestial rosary, and more especially
for the love she felt for the Temple which was
to rise in honor of Her rosary on this pagan
land of Pompei.

And even if this Image were removed the wonders of the Lord would still be the same.

Among the favors obtained while the second picture of Saint Catherine and the Virgin of the Rosary was in veneration it will suffice for me to recall one, which the reader already finds published and documented in the pamphlet, NOVENA TO THE MOST BLESSED VIRGIN OF THE ROSARY OF POMPEI, and also in the 3rd Year, page 34 of the monthly publication: THE ROSARY AND THE NEW POMPEI. I mean the blessing granted to myself in person, when on bringing this picture of the Nuptials of Saint Catherine into my room, the blessed Virgin restored me to life. This took place on the evening of the 18th of August 1879.

Whosoever should desire to-day to see this second picture will find it at the extreme end of the first dormitory of the little orphangirls. I wished that the Saint of the Benincasa family, the admirable teacher of all virtues who obtained for me from Mary the grace of my temporal life, should be a safe and sure guide to Heaven to all these poor orphans gathered together here one by one and entrusted to Her.

I thought no better place could be found for the painting, which was the means of the saving of my life, than here *in the midst of lonely innocence*, that composes the real crown of lilies and roses of the Queen of Victories of Pompei.

. .

Maldarelli kept the miraculous Image, to-day popularly known as the Virgin of Pompei, in his studio from June till August 1879.

He spared no pains to really make a devotional picture of it. He found the means of decreasing the size of the Virgin's head and of giving a certain air of refinement to the enormous face of the Saint Rose, at the same time thinning it down as much as possible; he also gave a gentler expression to the rough features of Saint Dominic and to the Babe he lent an air of vivacity which It to this day preserves.

But the trouble was, as has already been said, that the canvass was ruined. In order to renew it Comm. Maldarelli had recourse to one of the greatest artists in that line in Naples, Signor Francesco Chiariello, who then had and still has his studio in the Luperano Palace, Salita Museo.

I remember having paid Signor Chiariello sixty francs for the canvass alone. He with exquisite art, according to modern discoveries, withdrew from the painting the old and torn canvass, and substituted a new and much higher one, which fact enabled Comm. Maldarelli to add another palm of painting above the Virgin's head, space that was wholly lacking in the old picture. And this he did with such a perfect imitation of antique tints, as to make the whole appear, at a distance, the work of the same epoch and even author.

And so, the painting having been retouched the first time by the artist Galella in 1876, repainted by the celebrated Comm. Maldarelli in 1879, the face of the Virgin wholly altered, Saint Rose changed into Saint Catherine of Siena, even the old canvass removed and a new one substituted, the head of the Virgin and that of the Child crowned with a diadem of diamonds, her neck encircled with a necklace of precious gems, it will be seen that scarcely a trace of the old picture remains.

Thus exposed, surrounded by a frame of moulded bronze, that has cost *ten thousand* francs, with fifteen bronze medallions, encasing the fifteen mysteries of the Rosary, painted by

Paliotti, forming a crown around it, the painting has acquired such an artistic appearance, that the lovely face of the Virgin appears indeed like the *gently trembling morning star*.

However we still keep with the greatest pleasure the first pictures reproduced from that first homely painting.

The fortunate artist whom we first called to Pompei, was old Dolfino of Naples, who worked for the booksellers in the Via S. Biagio dei Librai, and was recommended to us by our friend, Sig. Salvatore Festa, the editor.

And yet those first reproductions and lithographic engravings, which to-day seem so hideous, were yet the objects of the greatest veneration. And we ourselves have seen them elegantly framed in gold and silver and venerated in the houses of noble families, more especially in the homes of those who were the first to receive us when we went around in Naples seeking to find subscribers for a *penny a month*.

But even after the second rennovation the Image was not yet in a condition to be photographed; and we still preserve, as an historic document, the first photographs taken, which suited no one in the world.

To be historically sincere and truthful we cannot attribute to the painter Maldarelli, nor yet would he attribute it to himself, a certain celestial expression, on the Virgin's face which all who to-day come to the Sanctuary notice and which inspires confidence, love and devotion at once. It is at the same time a ray of beauty, of gentleness, and of majesty that shines down from those eyes, making all who approach the Sanctuary with faith bend the knee before that old canvass while their heart beats with rapture. I am personally convinced that the Virgin by a visible portent has embellished Her own face.

And as many of us as are here concur in declaring that from the very day this painting was removed from the old and tumble-down Parish of the Most Holy Saviour, and placed in the new Chapel which forms a part of the great Sanctuary on the left, a certain beauty, a majesty and confidence inspiring sweetness are to be noticed on the features of the celestial Queen which most certainly were not to be seen before.

And if persons prefer to believe, what may also be the case, as the Virgin has no need of miracles, that this our manner of seeing

arises from the disposition of our hearts;
this fact will still remain incontrovertible
and out of doubt, as shown by daily proofs,
namely that persons of all nationalities, who
come here every day, behold in that Image
something which attracts and constrains admiration, not because of any artistic perfection, as this is certainly not a Madonna
painted by Raphael, but some secret, latent
power, which draws one, almost against one's
will, to kneel and pray.

Oh, yes! While praying before that Image,
one feels in one's soul the firm hope that
prayer will be answered, and such ineffable
bliss is enjoyed, *as who has never felt cannot
possibly understand.*

. .

This is the History of the miraculous Effigy
which is venerated in Valle of Pompei, centre
of the sighs, prayers, wishes and supplications
of thousands of catholics, who turn to our
blessed Queen with perfect confidence from
every part of Italy, Europe and the world.

———

CHAPTER V.

The first Miracle.

While during the first half of the month of February 1875, we were busy founding in Valle di Pompei the Society of the Most Holy Rosary and building a temporary Altar to the Virgin in order that the faithful might enjoy all the annexed Indulgences; such an extraordinary event had taken place in Naples, that from its very singularity in the course of a few days it was in the mouths of many, and even reached the ears of his Eminence the Cardinal, who was then Sisto Riario Sforza.

The rapid divulgation of this event also caused the news, that near the ruins of Pompei a church was going to be built to the real God, to circulate rapidly and find for its reception a large opening.

The event was really of such a nature as to be surprising: in fact it was a miracle, and the precise spot where it was said to have taken place was the house N. 62 in Via Tribunali.

But the strange part of it was that this certain something supernatural had taken place

in that house from the day that a certain
promise had been made to help in the building of some church which perhaps would
be erected in Pompei after who knows how
many years.

Those who bore witness to the fact were
not only a most distinguished family of Naples,
the Lucarelli, but also many other dwellers
in the same house; and especially Madam
Anna Maria Lucarelli, to day passed to a
better life, a woman of remarkable virtues, a
person of letters and an artist, a model for
all christian souls.

This strange event, which we are about to
relate was the first evident sign from Heaven,
which at an early period proved to all neapolitans the favor with which the celestial
Virgin looked upon the building of a church
sacred to Her on the ground so long held in
bondage by Satan. It was the first grace which
the Virgin granted to the lovers of her future
Temple.

In relating the fact to our readers we will
not depart by one word from the written
statement made out by Madam Anna Maria
Lucarelli and announced from all the pulpits
of that immense town.

Clorinda Lucarelli of Naples, a lovely child
of twelve years of age, but an orphan having
lost both parents, had since the month of
August 1874 been frightfully tormented with
horrible epileptic convulsions. Despite all the
remedies of the medicinal art, which were
ceaselessly applied, the disease progressed
in such a manner as to cause the greatest
sorrow and affliction to all the household.

Her loving aunt, Madam Anna Maria Lucarelli, who took the place of a tender mother
to the poor unfortunate child, wished to consult another of the most illustrious professors
of Naples, the celebrated Commendator Antonio Cardarelli. He agreed with the opinion of
other renowned physicians, namely that the
convulsions were of an epileptic nature. Nevertheless he prescribed a line of treatment,
but with regret pronounced the hard sentence
that he could give no sure hope of recovery.

The poor girl at this sad announcement becomes silent, grows pale and resignedly bows
her head.

But on the first day of May 1875 the girl's
aunt wished to take the child to the church

of Saint Nicholas Tolentino, where the miraculous Image of the Immaculate Conception of Lourdes is venerated, hoping that the Mother of God would save her poor niece from the insidious disease with which she was afflicted. She had her drink some of the miraculous water, had her inscribed in the registers of the Pious Mount of the Blessed Virgin, and prayed long and earnestly for the child's recovery. After which she returned home her heart full of faith and hope.

But God, for His high ends, thought fit to choose another time and another occasion to show the intercessory power of His Mother.

Clorinda grew worse and worse; the convulsions attacked her with greater frequency and intensity, till at last they followed each other every three or four days, and not unfrequently daily and at various intervals.

Then change of air was tried. But nevertheless despite the wholesome country air and the medicines constantly used she remained as she was for six months without the slightest change for the better. In fact the girl, worn out by the fruitless use of all medicinal remedies, without the knowledge of any one gave up every sort of treatment toward the end of November 1875.

Her loving aunt tired and worn out and fatigued by hopes deferred, after the suffering of so many woes, at last formed the heroic resolve of sending the beloved little invalid, under the care of a Daughter of Charity, to France to bathe in the prodigious waters of the Sanctuary of Lourdes, thus hoping to see her return cured. But how send away a child that required unceasing care and attention? For now the dreadful evil attacked the girl not only by day but also by night; and often she would fall to the ground with great force, often bleeding, and always frothing, and writhing her delicate little body, with constant danger to her life.

It was the day of the Feast of the Purification 1876: in the afternoon Clorinda suddenly escaped the vigil eye of her aunt, who, almost with a presentiment of some greater ill, went in search of her in fear and trembling. And she found her, horrible to think! near the well, with her head inside the bucket, having perhaps felt a desire to drink, and in that position taken with a most violent attack of convulsions, thus running the risk of suffocating herself and what is more precipitating into the well.

On the following day (the third of February) the poor child was tormented as she had never

been before. From morning till evening the
convulsions were so violent and so frequent,
that they rendered her almost insensible and
wholly incapable of even recognizing the
members of her family.

Her poor aunt was in a state of dejection
impossible to describe, when on that same
day, third of February, Countess De Fusco
entered the house, and during the course of
conversation happened to mention the fact
that a new church was to be built in Valle di
Pompei, dedicated to the Virgin of the Rosary.
And at the same time she informed her of certain singular events with which the Lord had
marked the beginning of this new undertaking.

She told her how in a few days a Brotherhood of the Rosary would be founded in
Pompei, and how an Image of the Virgin of the
Rosary would for the first time be exposed on
an Altar to attract the poor peasants, and instill
in their hearts the love for the celestial beads.
She also explained to her how forlorn was the
condition of those poor toilers of the land and
how great was their ignorance.

When the afflicted lady heard this tale she
felt newborn hope arise in her heart, and she
made a secret promise to help in the work with

all her power if only her niece should be cured;
what increased her hope too was the fact that
not only she herself but also her niece had for
several months been aggregated to the Third
Order of St. Dominic, and were for that reason
beloved daughters of the Virgin of the Rosary.

Mrs Anna Maria Lucarelli, moved by a faith
and a hope she had not felt for a long time,
subscribed her name, exclaiming:

— Countess, if the Virgin of the Rosary for
whom I feel an immense devotion will grant
me the grace of the recovery of this my niece,
I will be here at your service. I will myself
make the tour of the houses in Naples seeking
offerings for the church of Pompei. Here is
my offering, not of a cent a-month, but of ten
cents a month, and I pay down a whole year's
amount as pledge of the offering I will make
if my prayer is granted.

And the Queen of the heavenly Roses, Who
saw that the time was ripe for new manifesta-
tions of Her power to be shown to the perishing
world, or had perhaps, like at the marriage
feast in Canaan, by means of Her powerful
prayers obtained from Her divine Son the anti-
cipation of the hour of Her prodigies in the land
of dead Pagans, looked down from Heaven

upon that pious woman with the eyes of a Mother. And wonderful to relate! from the day on which Her Image was exposed to the pompeian people, from that memorable day of the 13th of February, when the Confraternity of the Rosary was erected in Pompei, from that day I say Clorinda was restored to complete health [1]).

Two famous Professors, the Messrs. Marzio Castronuovo and Salvatore Farina, who had attended Clorinda, were not at all reluctant to certify to the serious state of the young girl, to the perfect inutility of all medicines used and to the rapid, unhoped for transition from the most serious illness to complete recovery. Which recovery, not being based on any of the remedies recommended by Science, indeed in direct contradiction with all the opinions

---

1) This narrative is taken from the document written by Madam Anna Maria Lucarelli herself and dated April 3rd 1876, and read by Rev. Father Charles Rossi of the S. of I. in the month of May of that year 1876 in the Parish of Montesanto, and by the Rev. Father G. Altavilla of the S. of I. in the Parish of Saint Dominic Soriano the 24th of May of that same year; and announced by the Rev. Father de Felice, a Teatino monk in the church of Saint Gaetano in Naples, and published in the Periodical " LILIES TO MARY, „ IX issue, 15 June 1876.

of Science itself, could but force the minds of the doctors by strength of a logical deduction to admit the intervention of some supernatural power. Nothing more was required of them, and this was obtained as can clearly be seen from the following certificates.

1° « I, the undersigned, doctor in medicine and surgery, do hereby certify that Miss Clorinda Lucarelli as far back as the month of August 1874 began to suffer from undoubted paroxisms of central epilepsy, which repeated themselves at longer or shorter intervals up to the 3ʳᵈ *day of February of the year 1874* from which day up to the date here below affixed, *they have no longer manifested themselves*. I cannot omit to state that the diagnosis I made of the malady was completely ratified in a consultation held between myself and Professor Commendatore Antonio de Martino, and confirmed by Professor Cardarelli, and we all three decided upon and prescribed the most energetic curative farmaceutic and hygienic treatment, such as country air, chosen food, etc., but despite all these powerful medicinal remedies, the above mentioned epileptic paroxisms continued to be frequent and intense, during all the above-stated period, and more especially during the latter months their violence was extreme. — I sign this document in honor of truth.

Naples, May 18ᵗʰ 1876.

Signed: MARZIO CASTRONUOVO

2° I the undersigned, attendant Professor on Miss Clorinda Lucarelli, daughter of Professor Dominic Lucarelli deceased, and of about the age of twelve, do hereby certify that the said Miss had for several years been affected with epileptic convulsions, which could be attributed to no assignable cause, and which despite the most varied treatment continued to torment her at various times, by night as well as by day, till about four months ago. When *suddenly, without the use of any human remedies,* she passed from a state of extreme illness to a state of perfect health, which she is still enjoying to the surprise of all.

To this I certify on my honor and conscience, ready to confirm it with my oath.

Naples, June 4ᵗʰ 1876.

PROF. SALVATORE FARINA

CHAPTER VI.
The Neapolitan Nobility.

At that time it happened that the Countess met in the streets of Naples Mrs. Lucarelli, who was accompanying her two nieces, Laura and Clorinda, the latter in the best of health.

No sooner did the aunt see my wife, than with tears of joy in her eyes, she told the Countess all about the unexpected miracle, and:

« Here am I, » she added, inebriated with joy : — for two years have I made the round of all the churches in Naples, solliciting public prayers for the recovery of my dear Clorinda. Now I will return to all these churches to have public thanksgivings rendered to the Lord for this most special grace, and to have it attributed to the intercession of the Virgin of the Rosary who desires a church in Pompei. At this very moment I am going to tell what has happened to his Eminence the Cardinal Riario, to whom I have so often turned in my distress, acquainting him with my sorrow ».

What our joy was on hearing this news from the Countess upon her return home, the reader can readily imagine.

But when the first impulse of joy had subsided, and we began seriously to think the matter over, the reflection produced such a strong impression on us as to quite astound us.

— But is it possible? The Madonna thus bless a work so poorly and meanly begun!... And then, perform a miracle! and why?... for the rustic church of poor peasants!... It would therefore seem that She appreciates our good will... If this is so everything will proceed well. Perhaps the Madonna wishes us to begin the church immediately? Then we will begin it. —

All these considerations while on the one-hand they shed a ray of comfort on our spirit, on the other hand somewhat agitated us, as having the desire to do a great deal at one time we did not know on what first to lay our hand so as to proceed quickly.

— There is — thought we — but one safe and sure way: if only the aristocracy of Naples, which is wealthy and pious, would take a hand and an interest in the new work oh, then indeed would it go along on wheels. —

But how enter those homes where only titled people enter, or titled relatives, or titled strangers, introduced by other titled persons?

It is true we already had among our subscribers the Ladies Fonton, the noble and
pious Duchess of Casamassima, the Duchess
of Messanella, Lady Frances De Domenicis,
the friend of Mrs. Irbicella, the Duchess of
Montagnareale, Miss Raffaela Piria, the Duchess of Capracotta, and others belonging to
the Pious Union of Catherine Volpicelli: but
then the aristocracy of Naples is so very
numerous!.....

Nevertheless strengthened by that inner
force which proceeds from the faith and trust
in the supernatural we began to make the
rounds of the streets of Naples in order to
find subscribers for a *cent a month* to take
part in a work which Heaven already with
open miracles showed to appreciate.

The pious Duchess Mirelli was just returning from the meeting of Catherine Volpicelli.
The Countess, no sooner did she see her,
than she begged her to become a promulgator
of the new work and also sollicited her to indicate to us some powerful families to whom
to turn for the subscription of a cent a month.

— Do you wish to have numerous and good
addresses of wealthy and noble neapolitan
families? — answered the Duchess Mirelli,

Then turn to the Marchioness Filiasi di Somma whom you already know. It is her mother, the Princess del Colle, who has spread through Naples the devotion of the Fifteen Saturdays of the Rosary. The Marchioness is a saintly woman, wealthy, connected with the finest families in Naples, and what is more, given to building churches. I really could indicate to you no other person who would be as good a guardian angel and guide.

This advice appeared to us to be like the ray of sunlight that scatters the clouds.

Without losing time we directed our steps toward the Palace of Marchioness Filiasi.

It is sweet to remember after a lapse of nineteen years the conversation which took place that day and whence sprung the fact, that foremost among all the social classes, the aristocracy of Naples became the first pillar of origin and support of the great work God wished begun in Pompei.

The noble lady received us with a kind and benevolent familiarity, as though she had known us for a long time. But when she heard our project she was frank in expressing her opinion.

— You have — said she — undertaken a most difficult task. There are so many charities in

Naples !..... and such beautiful charities that
still are barely able to support themselves
because they all are upheld by the same persons. Now how do you wish to add another
one to the numberless ones already existing,
and especially the building of a church !... in
a desert country !... far from Naples... in fact
outside the Diocese of Naples. I must honestly
tell you that you will find it hard to succeed.
I after having spent more than fifty thousand
francs toward the erection of a church in Foggia,
have seen the whole thing left in suspense.
Moreover I know the nature of southerners;
they undertake new works with great fervor,
but then they tire because of the multiplicity
of the same and because new ones arise to
call their attention.

— Marchioness — answered we — we have
already presented all these difficulties to our
holy Bishop of Nola. But do you know what
he answered? « You are egotists: you are only
thinking of yourselves and your own time.
Churches are not built in one generation. Saint
Peter's in Rome and Saint Peter's in Peters-
burg were only completed after three centuries.
You have the merit of beginning; others after
fifty years will have the merit of finishing ».

The Marchioness, who was truly good, shrugged her shoulders, and added:

— To satisfy you and so as to have a little merit myself, I subscribe my name. But with only a cent a month you will do nothing; ladies at least should subscribe for fifty centimes (ten cents) a month, and I to set the example shall subscribe for half a franc every month.

After which the Marchioness had her daughter-in-law and her son, the Marquis Luigi Filiasi, subscribe, as also her german governess and other members of her family.

Before leaving she turned to us, saying:

— However let me give you one piece of advice. Call in no architect for this work which only counts on penny subscriptions and will last dear knows how many years, otherwise the architect's fee alone will absorb half your capital. I know this by experience. After having spent many thousand francs on the church and convent of F. Ludovico of Casoria on the Tondo of Capodimonte (Naples) all work now has been suspended, but what is worse poor Fr. Ludovico is in litigation with the architect because this latter wishes to exact his fee.

— My dear Marchioness, — said I smiling « and who could think of calling an architect?

Moreover being a church for peasants, to be built in a desert land, there will be no need of architects. We will do all things ourselves. I have already thought of what I shall do: I shall go with my mason to some near town and look at some church, we will take the necessary measurements with some twine, and then we will lay the foundations. —

When I had ceased speaking, she gave us a quantity of her visiting-cards, telling us at the same time the names and addresses of many of her relatives and friends, to whom to present them in her name. And she had her own butler accompany us to the house of the Count of Gigliano, and to the residences of the Marchioness of Rende, the Duke of Bivona, the Princess of Torella, the Duchess of Salve, the Princess of Gerace, the Princess of Angri, where we named Miss Josephine Anastasio promoter, of the Duchess of Eboli, the Duchess of Gallo, the Marchioness Ruffo, the Marchioness Calenda, the Marchioness of Guidamandri and others.

And so through these noble ladies we were introduced to other families of note, as through the excellent Duke of Capracotta, between whom and ourselves there existed a brotherly friendship, we had the good fortune to become acquainted with such pious and distinguished persons as the Duke of Paganica, the Count de La Tour, the Duchess of Mayo, the Duchess of Tora, the Marchioness of Latiano Mayo, the Marchioness Piscicelli, the Duke of San Vito, the Marchioness of Salandra, the Countess of Balsorano, the Marchioness of d'Ayala Valva, whose niece Miss Maria d'Ayala, is to this day fulfilling the sweet duties of promoter of the Madonna of Pompei. At the same time we were so very fortunate as to interest in the incipient church of Pompei, through ways wholly providential the Duchess of Laurenzana, the Countess Gaetani di Laurenzana, the Marchioness Bonelli, the Marchioness of Saint Eramo, the Princess Pignone del Carretto and that english gentlelady Miss Mackleod, the instructress of Miss Amelia Colonna, the daughter of Prince Colonna of Stigliano, who now is among the most fervent promoters of the Sanctuary of Pompei.

And this is how, most certainly by divine will and counsel, the neapolitan aristocracy was elected by the Queen of Heaven to take a prominent part in the first beginnings of the Sanctuary of Pompei.

It is not for us to scrutinize the ways of Providence; but one fact impresses itself most forcibly on our minds, now that nineteen years have passed, a fact that constitutes a distinguishing feature of this Sanctuary. It may perhaps be owing to this divine disposition, that ever since the annual festivals in the Valle of Pompei began, a certain solemn and noble gravity, such as is fitted to divine worship, has always been observed, even on the occasion of the greatest solemnities, as the populace of Naples, good and full of heart and generosity though it is, yet still by nature noisy and fun loving, did not take part in them; and so that religious demeanor, so contrary to all noise and clamorous feasts, has become, by force of example, the habit and custom of this and neighboring people. Hence it arises, that despite the immense crowd of people, there is always a profound and religious silence reigning in the Sanctuary, the silence of adoration and of heartfelt prayer.

———

CHAPTER VII.

The first Thornpricks.

A worthy friend of ours, Professor Giuseppe
de Bonis, Parish Priest of Vallecorsa, has
written, in the form of a romance, the first
little episodes that occurred on our beginning
the work of God here in Pompei, and has named
the book « POMPEIAN ROSES AND THORNS » [1]).
With this title he alluded to a maxim, the truth
of which is constantly being proven in the
holy and civilizing work that Mary is carrying
on in this Valley, which is: that there is no
triumph without a battle, as there is no rose
without thorns. This same principle we will
keep before us in weaving the history of
the Sanctuary, in which it will find its constant affirmation. In the very Introduction we
clearly stated this truth, writing as we did:
« There has been no triumph of the Sanctuary of Pompei without adversity, nor glory
that was not preceded by humiliation. Our
great consolations have constantly been

[1] *Giuseppe de Bonis,* POMPEIAN ROSES AND THORNS. Valle
di Pompei, Editing School of Typ. of Bartolo Longo 1887.

preceded by great bitternesses; but in all our
hard trials we have been sustained and strengthened by the loving hand of the Lady of this
Valley, whose title is the Queen of Victories. »

This premitted let us start out to narrate
our first trials.

The first days of March of that year 1876
arrived. I who had seen the good will and
interest of several noble families of Naples
aroused in the course of only one month, and
had seen the Virgin most effectively strengthen
our first steps by a most evident miracle, rendered a thing of public note in that town; felt
impatient to begin the building of this church,
especially as I felt an inner stimulus which
no longer gave me peace or rest.

— When I shall have begun to erect the
walls of the Temple of Pompei — so thought
I, — there will be no one who will refuse to
lend me a helping hand. —

To tell the truth in the strong ardor of my
desire, no obstacle appeared to me insur-
mountable; and ignorant as I was of such
like undertakings I certainly believed that the
Evil One, who so loves to oppose all his ar-
tifices to the works of God, could not conquer
the fervor of my heart nor the strength of my

proposals. But I very early found out by **sad** experience, how **great** an energy Satan displayed to hinder the building of a Temple to his arch-enemy, Jesus Christ, and also what his power still was over this land of Pompei where for centuries his rule had been peaceful and unassailed.

We will see what troubles and contrarieties the great Enemy raised from the very outstart, and what bitternesses he conjured up to discourage us from our enterprise [1]).

---

1) Many, perhaps even among those who call themselves catholics, who go to Mass and observe other external practices belonging to divine worship, will wonder on reading this part of the history how openly I attribute to the demon an active and direct part in the operations of man. Yet they must well know, that the Bible, Theology and Ecclesiastical History all teach very clearly how the fallen angels disturn man from doing good works; and how the evil spirits, in order to oppose the good intentions of men, who allow themselves to be docily guided by the inspirations of holy Angels, gather together to take counsel and make horrible plans, calculating the time, the nature, the natural tendencies of the person they wish to assail, his condition and age, and thus they lay traps and prepare their nets long before they make a violent attack upon him to conquer him and bring him under their dominion. To some who because of the nature of their of life or studies, are reluctant to admit the

It is well known that before building an edifice the foundations must first be laid, and you c annot lay a foundation when you have not the n ecessary plot of ground. So we began to look around for a plot of ground on which to build.

The reader will remember how in November 1875 the Bishop of Nola, looking out of the

---

intervention of the supernatural in the actions of man, this theory may appear fantastic or the dream of a lightly balanced mind. These *Naturalists*, who do not believe in the super or extra-natural, such as the intervention of good and bad angels, who deride the mistic science as middle-century rubbish, and consider the apparitions of angels good or bad to be merely the effect of fantasy or hysterics, do believe, in order to explain certain praeter-human facts, in certain scientific, or arbitrary psichiatric, theories; I mean to say in Magnetism, lucid sonnabulism, hypnotism and the work of Mediums. It really arouses our pity to see men of mind and vast knowledge, become excited, meet in conferences, and publish long articles in the papers, trying to demonstrate hypnotism to be a science. However we intend to luminously demonstrate all this in another work, so the Lord grant us life. And then we will be better able to answer certain subscribers to our Journal, who often ask us whether Hypnotism and Spiritualism be a progress of the natural Sciences and the human mind, and whether in such an hypothesis, it be allowable for social and individual wellfare, to try experiments and follow its principles.

window of the De Fusco house and stretching
forth his arm, had pointed out in an inspired
manner, the spot where the new temple was
to rise, namely in the centre of the Valley,
by the side of the old Parish of the Most Holy
Saviour, in the province of Naples.

So our first steps were directed toward
finding the proprietor of the land adjoining
the Parish. Having found out that it belonged
to a gentleman of Boscoreale, we sent to him
the Rev. Father Gennaro Federico, to act in
the matter. But despite all the going back
and forth it was impossible to come to any
settlement as his price appeared to us to be
too exorbitant.

One evening, as we were gathered together
in the little house at Valle, the Countess, the
Rev. Federico and other friends, and myself,
we talked the whole matter over with no
slight preoccupation, and were in great doubt
as to what to do, whether to consent to pay
the exorbitant price or to turn to the proprietors of other plots of ground.

But on the following morning lo and behold
our faithful companion in the work, the Rev.
Gennaro Federico, come to us, pale and excited, saying:

— A most horrible vision came to me early this morning and thus spoke to me: — How can you thus throw away the money which is the blood of the poor? Leave that proprietor and go to that *pious man* (and it pointed to a field lying to the east of the De Fusco dwelling). He will give you the land on which to build the church without any compensation [1]).

---

1) Even some catholics at the mere sound of the words *spirits* or *vision* feel alarmed. But Saint Thomas and Dante write that toward morning, when our imagination is quiet, good or bad angels more clearly impress their inspirations on our minds. Moreover all the Teachers of Asceticism, among whom St. John of the Cross, Saint Catherine of Siena, Saint Theresa, St. Laurence Giustiniani, St. Catherine of Genua, the Jesuit Francis P. Surin, and many others, say neither to despise and reject them utterly at first sight, nor yet to accept them; but to examine and distinguish whether it be a natural event, or some diabolical or divine intervention. We read in Genesis and the Book of Kings of the appearance of phantoms and diabolical spirits, who have spoken to men', beginning with the first man who held colloquy with Satan under the guise of a serpent. Nor must this surprise us. The History of the Fathers in the Desert shows that the evil spirits are wont with their wiles and terrors to try and overthrow the inspirations of good Angels. And from the Book of Tobias we learn that a·demon tormented the young maid Sarah, and that the Archangel Raphael freed her from that nefarious

We will not here enter upon any discussion as regards this vision; we merely mention it for the sake of historical precision, because it really caused us loss of time, of strength and of money. This much is certain that in the condition in which we found ourselves, we were anxious to try to come to terms with other proprietors.

So what between the perplexity and the vague hope of obtaining gratuitously the much desired land, we ran in search of the pious gentleman of Boscoreale.

He really was a pious and agreeable man; he received us with all the courtesy possible and with sincere cordiality. He told us that

---

spirit, relegating it to the desert. We likewise learn both from the Old and New Testament, as also from the History of the Church, that good Angels have lent their services to man. Thus did they eat with Abraham, wrestle with Jacob, visit with Jedeon, serve the son of Tobias, minister to Christ in the desert, break the bonds of and open the doors to Saint Peter and lead him through the streets; they ploughed for St. Isidore, and worked for St. Omobono; they sustained the blessed Mary d'Oigne; assisted St. Coletta when infirm, and served St. Liduina and others for thirty years. (See EPITOME HISTORIAE ANGELORUM by Father Boniface Costantino of the S. O. J.).

the land was not his but belonged to his wife
who at the time was absent; but he led us
to hope for the best.

Bright and happy we flew back to Valle di
Pompei to carry the good news to the Countess and the principal inhabitants of the valley. The building plot was at least sure, and
perhaps would be given gratuitously. The
temple was no longer to rise opposite the De
Fusco dwelling in the province of Naples, but
on the east side of the same, in the province
of Salerno. Little mattered it to us whether
in this or in that province, so only we could
at last see all these poor peasants gathered
for the first time in a spacious sacred edifice
to listen to the word of God and to enjoy the
sacred cerimonies of the catholic church.

That day was a day of rejoicing in Valle.

But several days passed and no answer
came from the lady proprietress; but finally
it did arrive; the lady, though with great charm
of manner, *did not consent.*

We were disconcerted: we did not know
to whom to turn, when the Countess came
forward with a proposal of her own.

— The land to the west of this dwelling —
she said — I hold, it is true, in common with

my younger children De Fusco; but still I do hold a certain part, which I gladly renounce for the building of the church.

The solution of all difficulties seemed thus to be found. The much desired church was therefore not to rise either opposite the Parish of the Saviour as the venerable Bishop of Nola had counseled, nor yet to the right as proposed by the Rev. Federico, but on the western-side, on a vast area, with its entrance on the provincial highway Naples-Salerno.

And immediately, carried away by indescribable joy, we went to visit the proposed site; and we began to hastily plant pickets, drawing thus the design of a vast church with an ample vestryroom, with a dwelling for the rector, and a thousand other little details.

— Let us write to the Bishop, — said the Countess — every obstacle has been removed, every difficulty overcome.

This advice was immediately followed, and the Bishop lost no time in answering. But he was opposed to the project.

—How can you build a church,—he observed with great prudence—on a land not properly divided and partly belonging to minors. When they become of age they would be entitled to assert their rights and to take the land and the church built on it.

The prudent advice of the Bishop decided us to again change our plans. But our minds, offuscated by so many oppositions, were completely in the dark.

———

CHAPTER VIII.

Latiano and Pompei.

But not even these contrarieties sufficed. While I was feeling somewhat discouraged, I received on the twelfth day of that same March three dispatches from Latiano in Terra d'Otranto, calling me thither immediately as my good Mother had been taken with such a violent attack on the brain, that her life was despaired of.

Very often she had been attacked by severe cerebral forms brought on by palpitation of the heart, that had threatened her days, but this last one had come to end them.

It was a great blow to me to know that her condition was such as not to be able to receive the last sacraments of the church nor yet sign her will on which depended the good harmony of two families.

Her friends and physicians of Naples, hearing the nature of the disease, gave up all hope.

I then rushed to my little church of the Third Order, at Porta Medina; and there at

the altar of the Virgin, where five years before
I had received the white scapular of the Third
Order, I begged the Mother of Mercies, to once
again save my family from so great a misfortune. She read in my inmost soul my firm
purpose never to abandon the blessed work
of her church in Pompei.

The following morning I went to Pompei
to see the Rev. Federico and to inform him
of my great misfortune and also to tell him
to defer any negotiations regarding the acqui-
sition of a plot of ground on which to build
the church till my return.

But there was another scene of sorrow
awaiting me in Pompei.

I entered the home of the Federicos, almost
dark for want of light, and I beheld that
numerous family gathered together, with tears
in their eyes, in the perfect silence of cons-
ternation.

Giuseppe Federico, the father, at 67 years
of age, oppressed by a most violent fever,
having lost all power of speech, his mind
wandering and his eyes almost glazed, was
dying from an attack of pleuro peri-pneumo-
nia, and was unable to receive the sacraments
or sign his will.

The attending doctor, having exhausted all human remedies, had reluctantly informed the family that all hope was lost.

At that sight, struck by the similarity of the two cases, and remembering at the same time that on that very day, the 13th of March, a full month had elapsed since we had exposed the Image of the Rosary to veneration in Pompei and founded the Society of the Most Holy Rosary,

—It is strange—I murmured in a low voice —Not one, but two dying. On the very same day my Mother, and the Father of my only companion in Pompei in the work of the new Church are brought to death's door. Could it be possible that the Virgin of the Rosary should grant her favors to others and deny them to those who are so anxious to work for Her glory?—

I spoke a few words of hope and comfort to the afflicted family and also revealed to them the fact that my home in Latiano had been visited by the same trial. Immediately the other son, also a priest, Romualdo Federico, made his dying father pronounce a vow in favor of the new church. And the latter not only promised to offer 425 francs but also to help gratuitously in the work of construction.

This done I left immediately. I reached Latiano on the evening of the following day. I found my Mother still alive, but deprived of speech and motion; nevertheless I did not abandon all hope. First of all I besought her to repeat together with me the Hail Mary and to do her utmost to articulate the sweet words. And oh wonderful to say; by degrees as she proceeded to stammer forth the words, her tongue became loosened.

After the lapse of five days, and exactly on the 19th day sacred to the Patriarch St. Joseph, my Mother had signed her will, had received the Holy Communion, and was happily seated at table together with all her sons, who had come there from various parts of the country to weep over her dead body.

The same thing had taken place in Pompei in the Federico home. The very evening I left there, when everything seemed to prognosti_ cate the last and fatal stages of Giuseppe Federico's malady, the malady disappeared; the fever ceased, life reappeared, and the following day he recited with his sons the Rosary of Mary. On the same day, the 19th of

March the Federico family were celebrating
in Pompei the recovery of the father [1]).

---

1) These two homogeneous and contemporaneous facts
are certified to and signed by the following witnesses:
Father Romualdo Federico — Father Gennaro Federico --
Giuseppa, Angiola, Pasquale, Rosa Federico — Lucia de
Vivo — Carlo Izzo — Michele Pastore — Giovanni Cirillo,
Pastor — Antonio di Palma, Priest — Bartolo Longo,
Lawyer.

CHAPTER IX.

In Francavilla Fontana.

« The Puglie! Who does not love that generous region, the cradle of a people so ardent
and yet so moderate; that land so fertile in
its wealth of olive-groves and of fine vines
and splendid wheat, that have caused it to
be named the *golden goblet* of the kingdom
of Naples. Ever since a child have I learned
to love that dear province, called by Regaldi
in his poems the Bersheba of Italy [1]. »

The Puglie gave me the first breath of material and moral life. I was born in Latiano,
in the Province of Lecce, a little town of seven
thousand inhabitants; it is entirely surrounded
by gardens and vineyards, and lies in a smiling
plain beneath a lovely sky, and is not far
distant from Brindisi. My father entrusted my
education, when I was six years of age, to
the Rev. Fathers of the Pious Schools, who at
that time had a flourishing college in Francavilla Fontana.

---

[1] De Bonis, Pompeian Roses and Thorns, Valle di
Pompei, 1887.

Francavilla is a large town of over twenty thousand inhabitants, with broad streets, and numerous buildings and churches and convents and hospitals and a college for young men of good families. Ever since I resided there it was one of the most cultivated towns of the province of Lecce. And considering the long time I lived there, a period of ten years which I passed in college, both from an intellectual and moral point of view I may call Francavilla my second home.

— Now since I am here in the Puglie — thought I to myself when I saw my Mother again restored to life — it will be well if I try and make my stay here fruitful in help for the Temple of Pompei. —

So I determined to make a trip to neighboring towns to spread the glories of the Rosary and to seek offerings and subscriptions for the new Temple.

The first town to which I turned my steps was my second home, Francavilla.

I even remember the very day; it was the 24th of March of that memorable year 1876, the vigil of the great feast in which all the world celebrates the divine Motherhood of Mary, the feast of the Annunciation.

I had not been to Francavilla for eighteen years. It is true that I had several old friends and college companions among the aristocracy of the place, but I was truly afraid that a new generation, grown up during my long absence under the modern atmosphere of civil strife and decrease of faith, would receive my proposition of building a new church more than two hundred miles distant with the utmost coldness.

I thought it prudent to go first of all to one of the noblest and wealthiest families of the aristocracy of Francavilla, to Commendatore Luigi Foresio, whose son John had been my companion in college.

The warm reception granted me comforted me not a little. I then told them of the reasons of my trip thither, and I asked for a list of families to whom to apply for aid in my difficult undertaking, without having to fear a humiliating refusal.

— Fortunately — answered Commendatore Foresio, — our Bishop of Oria is residing here. He is very wealthy, a millionaire; and a short while ago he gave one hundred and fifty thousand francs to the Passionist Fathers of Manduria to build there a church and convent from their very foundations.

At this joyful piece of news my heart expanded; and my mind was comforted by a kind of hope that if the Bishop of my Diocese had given one hundred and fifty thousand francs to build a church in Manduria, already so well supplied with sacred edifices, how could he but receive well one who was a native of his Diocese and was intending to build a church in a place where God was so little known and loved?

It was therefore resolved that my first visit should be to my Bishop. I went to his palace, and asked to be received.

— Whom shall I announce? — asked a servant.

— Name the lawyer Bartolo Longo of Latiano. —

After a few moments there appeared the venerable figure of an old man, tall and thin, who looking me full in the face, remained standing at a certain distance. Perhaps he did not like my appearance; my pale face and my hurried, excited speech perchance gave him the idea that I might be a doubtful personality. Noble old man! In his long life he had undoubtedly experienced human perversity more than once; and it is not to be wondered

at if feebleness and his eighty years of life
had made him cautious; moreover he was
hard of hearing.

— What do you wish? Who are you? — he
inquired with a certain reserve.

— I am lawyer Bartolo Longo of Latiano, —
answered I loudly so as to be understood — I
have lived in Naples for many years. Providence has led me to Pompei. The Bishop of
Nola has encouraged me to build a church
there for the poor peasants who are in need
of one. First of all I have come to you, Excellency, as to my Pastor, to ask for your
help in such a holy work. —

Naturally, being obliged to speak loudly so
as to make myself understood, I became red
in the face, not to mention a certain delicacy
on my part in asking for money.

But those few words were enough to strengthen that holy man in the belief that I had
come there to impose upon him; beside which
I not only had come before his presence without
his knowing me at all, but I also spoke in a
decided manner. So to give me an answer
which would confound me and prevent me
from going any further he said with signifi-
cance:

— You have mentioned the Bishop of Nola? I know him; he is wealthy; he alone can build a church. Go, go to him.

— But listen to me, Excellency.

— Go — he said raising his voice.

With lowered head, discomfited, confused, discouraged, I muttered a salutation, took off my hat and went down stairs.

— I have begun well. If the Bishop has treated me like a thief, others can but have me arrested and consigned to the Carabineers.

I hesitated whether to return immediately to Latiano, or whether to stop over that day and the next in Francavilla to try my fortune still further with the inhabitants, and to seek out my old friends and acquaintances. Humiliated and discouraged as I felt I decided to remain, so as not wholly to have lost my journey and have returned to my old home in vain.

I returned to Comm. Foresio, and told him of my miserable failure.

— There is certainly some mistake here — he exclaimed. — Our Bishop is not a man to receive you in this manner. Let the Mayor, who is a relation of yours speak to him and he will change his mind. —

I followed this advice, and the Mayor, Cavaliere Giovanni Galante, brought me in response a sum of twenty francs from the Bishop's brother, accompanied by many excuses [1]).

However what between that going back and forth and a certain discouragement that had taken hold of me in consequence of my first experience that day slipped by without any further event worthy of note. That little episode taught me that if I intended making a tour of the families I must do so in the company of some one who was known. I must therefore find a friend who not only knew me, but who also had the courage and the sangfroid to present himself to all the best families of the town without fear of an unpleasant reception. All through the evening and the night I was in deep distress of mind.

I arose two hours before day-break. I was a guest in the house of the Mayor, Chevalier

---

1) To render full justice to the family of that venerable Bishop by whom I was not then known I must add that his niece, Mrs. Margaret Carissimo, is at the present moment erecting in Francavilla Fontana at her own expense a chapel to the Blessed Virgin of Pompei. Wonderful disposition of Providence.

Giovanni Galante, which house was not far distant from the largest church in Francavilla.

The festive sound of the great bells pealing forth the Angelus of the morning announced the anniversary of that blessed day when the archangel Gabriel saluted the pure Maid of Nazareth and announced unto her the great Mystery of the Incarnation.

It was still dark. But at the joyful music of those bells my heart opened anew to a feeling of happiness and hope, and to a desire of prayer. I prostrated myself, I greeted the Virgin, and told her how I too that day needed an angel in human form to be my companion in announcing to the good people of Francavilla the glad tidings of her work in Pompei. And that Temple, though I did not know it then, was itself really a mystery; a mystery of love, and a mystery of mercy shown by Mary to this our century, which the more light it receives, the darker it grows. Some day, not more than seven years from that time the Temple of Pompei was to be the cause of the greatest blessings and benedictions to that same town of Francavilla, as will be told in due time.

I went out to attend the morning Mass celebrated before dawn. I found myself among an immense crowd which not only filled the large chapel of the Virgin of the Fountain, where Mass was being celebrated, but also the whole right nave. During the celebration I besought the Virgin to allow me to meet with some fit companion. I then suddenly remembered an old friend, by name Louis Salerno, who was a public teacher, and hence known in town, and a man of unbiased mind and good religious principles.

— But where — thought I — can I find him at this hour? And who knows if he is still in Francavilla? —

When lo and behold, on coming out of church, jostled and hustled by the crowd, I heard my name called. I turned, and oh, what joy, I recognized the very Louis Salerno of whom I had been thinking during Mass.

— How come you to be here? — this was the mutual question we exchanged. He then told me that it had never been his habit to leave his house at that hour to listen to that early Mass but that on that particular morning he had felt impelled to do so, he did not himself know why.

Taking him aside I said to him without any introductions, as frank people always do: — See here, matters stand in this and this wise. You can help me. —

— With all my heart am I ready to help you. I will not leave you one moment.

My friend kept his word, and with him I began a tour of the town, entering all the homes of well to do families, and arousing their pity by my description of the miseries of Valle di Pompei, and at the same time exciting in them a desire to taste of the inestimable sweetness and the sublime beauties of the Rosary of Mary.

I must confess this to the glory of the town of Francavilla, people of every description placed in my hands the offerings of their charity, and among all of them I remember certain persons who professed themselves atheists and unbelievers. May this their generosity be the first ring in the chain which shall draw them near to Truth, and the foretaste of that peace which alone is found in the love of God and in the love of Her who is His Mother. And the Virgin of the Rosary will never forget those dear and good Francavillians who were the first in the three Puglie to concur in the holy work of Pompei.

At the end of two days I had collected in Francavilla Fontana the snug little sum of four hundred and ninety francs. In those early days, and in so short a time, it was a fabulous sum.

———

CHAPTER X.

Unexpected Help from Heaven.
Miraculous Recovery of Madam Vastarella.

Having made a tour of the town of Mesagne, not to mention my little Latiano, with excellent results, as also several other places in the Puglie, I returned to Valle di Pompei.

On my return, the priest Gennaro Federico, came to meet me with open arms, himself full of joy.

— There is — said I — no time to lose now. We must absolutely purchase the necessary plot of ground to begin the building of the Temple as soon as possible. We must once more open negotiations with the proprietor of that piece of land which was pointed out to us by the Bishop, and which lies in the Province of Naples, adjoining the Parish. —

— But the proprietor is obdurate. He demands no less than one thousand seven hundred francs for three hundred feet of ground. So what will we have left on which to begin the foundations? —

— Let us turn to our holy Bishop for advice:
the voice of God will speak to us through
the mouth of our Superior. —

. .

It was the beginning of the spring of the
year 1876. A most brilliant sunlight followed
the cold and wet days of March, and called
into new life the humble field-flowers and
clover, which cover the fertile country round
Valle di Pompei like a green carpet.

It was the morning of the third of April.
The Countess and I were in Naples, and were
issuing from the little church of the Rosary
at Porta Medina comforted by the bread of
Angels, and ready to rebegin with activity
our tour through the most pious families of the
town. I turned toward Toledo [1]). The Countess,
accompanied by Miss Ernestina Freda; took a
hack and turned towards the Via di Chiaja [2]);
but, because of some little trouble with the
cabman, she changed her mind and had him
drive towards the Via of Capodimonte.

---

1) The principal thoroughfare of Naples.
2) The aristocratic street of Naples.

The two ladies having reached the first square, which comes after the ascent in the street, stopped before the Mautone Palace at Saint Theresa, N. 81.

They had heard that a very charitable and pious lady lived there; but they only knew her surname, Vastarella. It was their intention to ask her to subscribe to the church of Pompei. That palace had several staircases.

— Where does Madam Vastarella live? — they asked of the porter.

This personage with spanish gravity and without moving waved his hand in the direction of the staircase on the left hand side.

The two ladies began their ascent, but on no door could they find the name Vastarella inscribed. They continued their way up, and on the landing of the second floor they read the word: Miccio. But the door was open, and a great many people, some consternated and some sorrowful, appeared to be going back and forth.

— Please — asked the two ladies of another who was entering — can you kindly tell us where to find Madam Vastarella? —

— She does not live here; you must take the stairway opposite. —

—And to think the porter directed us here!...

— Oh yes — exclaimed the lady — he is right. Madam Vastarella is here to day, because her daughter is dying. —

At such an unexpected announcement the Countess and Miss Freda were about to retrace their steps. It was too evident that they would have been considered most indiscreet and annoying had they tried to speak of the plans of some future work to a mother weeping over her dying daughter

Fortunately at that very moment a young miss came out. Her face was flushed and wet with tears. She was another daughter of Madam Vastarella, by name Annina.

When she heard the name of the Countess, which was well known to her as that of a promoter of the Heart of Jesus, thinking that the two ladies had come for the purpose of finding associates to the Confraternity of the Sacred Heart, she invited them to enter, as it seemed to her that they had been sent by Our Lady to soothe the dreadful sorrow of her mother with words of faith. And so all three entered the inner rooms, where a dreadful scene was being enacted.

A young lady of twenty two years, who was

in a delicate condition, black in the face and emitting the dread gurgling sound, forerunner of death, having lost consciousness and speech, was writhing in the most horrible contorsions, distending and then rolling herself up in such a manner as to leave no hope either for herself or the child she was bearing.

The young lady's name was Concetta Vastarella, daughter of Giovanni and of Madam Louise Vastarella, née Passaro, and she was married to Signor Vincenzo Miccio. She had been quite despaired of by the doctors, among whom were the distinguished Chevalier Novi, and illustrious Professor Cantani.

Her parents, her husband and all the family had vowed themselves to God and the Blessed Virgin with many prayers and promises to obtain her recovery.

It was near noon, and the state of the patient was rapidly approaching its fatal end; in fact Doctor Novi had candidly stated that the next attack of convulsions would end all.

It was thought wise to have her father, who was worse than afflicted, completely prostrated, leave the room; and to call the confessor little as he could do for a soul laboring under such a suspension of intellect.

. .

It was at this juncture that the Countess entered the home of the Miccios.

Without even looking at the patient, she asked to be introduced to the sorrowing Mother.

Madam Vastarella was seated on a lounge, buried in the deepest affliction, and dissolved in tears.

As soon as the poor lady saw the Countess and her companion, she exclaimed weeping:

— I have vowed myself to the Heart of Jesus and to the Immaculate of Lourdes; but all in vain!...

The Countess then gently told her that she venerated both of those sacred Devotions as most miraculous, but that she had not come for that, but for a new church to the Virgin of the Rosary to be built in Valle di Pompei.

And briefly stating all the extraordinary events that had transpired up to that day, beholding the desolation of that family, seeing the tears of the friends and of the mother, Madam Louise Passaro, beside herself with grief, and considering on the other hand by

14

what a strange concatenation of circumstances she came to be in that house, where she had never been known nor knew anybody, and where she was not even intending to come that morning, having first devised to go to a certain house in Chiaja; on the impulse of the ˙moment, without even looking at the patient, and with great faith, she uttered before all present these words:

— I promise that the Virgin of the Rosary, for whose church I am tramping around, and for whom I now find myself in this house, will grant you your request, as she already has done to two other families. —

Then a gentleman, who was perhaps the Doctor, spoke up:

— Those are very bold words: the patient is already near her end and the case is very desperate. —

— Exactly because it is desperate — answered the Countess — the Virgin can show her power.

She then invited them to make a promise of some small amount for the new church of Valle di Pompei and also to recite the fifteen mysteries of the Holy Rosary, concluding with these words:

— Have faith. —

— Ah, — answered the sorrowing mother of the dying girl, — at this present moment I am broken in spirit; I have no more faith. All night long I have called on the Sacred Heart of Jesus and made promises, but without any result. I have made a vow to Our Lady of Sorrows, miraculous protectress of our family; candles have been sent to the Virgin of Lourdes. In vain; now I am dazed; make any promise you will for me yourself. —

— Well — answered the Countess — promise, that if you obtain your desire, you will let all the world know of it, and will make out a full and true statement of the facts. —

— Not only will we write about it — responded the afflicted parent, — but we will come to Valle di Pompei to tell our tale to every one, on the day that the Bishop shall lay the corner-stone of the new church.

Then all went to see the patient.

She was in a bath, her lips black, her teeth clenched, her eyes staring, her body writhing in horrible contorsions, an ice-bag on her head, completely deprived of consciousness or feeling.

The Countess and Miss Freda left the house

in sorrow. The Countess returned home greatly agitated and strongly impressed by her
recent experience. She hastened to relate to
all the members of her family the strange
thing which had occurred that morning; how
instead of going to Chiaja as she had intended she had gone to Capodimonte, how she
had mistaken the dwelling of the Miccio family for that of Madam Vastarella; how she
had found herself in a house of tears and had
seen with her own eyes a young mother in a
pitiful condition, and how she had allowed a
promise to escape her lips, sure that the Virgin would perform a miracle for the love of
her new church of Pompei. The doubt, the hope,
the fear of an uncertain result, communicated
themselves to the spirits of all of us. How
were we to know whether the Virgin would
really look with an eye of favor on the strong
presumption and over confidence of the Countess in promising a miracle in her name?

— Madam Miccio's malady — we reasoned —
is one that does its work quickly. The Countess left her in a most desperate state; hence
the day will not pass without either her death
or a miracle taking place. —

— What a grand thing it would be for the

work of Pompei, if this other miracle were to take place here in Naples!...

The bells of the neighboring convent of Saint Monica were ringing to Vespers.

Our home that year was in Via Salvator Rosa, on the square San Efrem Nuovo, in the palace of Signor Passaro, N° 290. That house occupies a dear place in our memories for it was the cradle of the holy work of the New Pompei; and it was in that house that we received the first announcement that the Virgin of the Rosary had performed *a miracle* in Naples for love of her new church to be built in Pompei. I remember to a nicety that the first news of the first miracle was brought to the house personally by a very pious lady, by the Duchess Albertini Sozi-Carafa.

— By this time — exclaimed the Countess, — Madam Miccio has either died or has been saved. We must find a way out of this uncertainty. —

And having called an old and faithful servant, Domenico Ostuni by name, she said to him:

— Go to the Mautone Palace at Saint Theresa. Do not enter: look first to see whether the portal be half closed. That will be the sign

that the lady is dead. And without entering
or speaking to any-one return immediately.
But if the portal be wide open enter and in-
quire of the porter as to the state of health
of Madam Concetta Miccio Vastarella.

The servant obeyed his mistress to the
letter.

It was an half-hour of agitation and heart-
throbs for us.

But who can tell the exultation, the joy, the
tears of gladness, the cries of happiness, when
Domenico, having returned, said to us: — I
found the portal open, and the porter told me
that Madam Concetta was *quite well?* —

We were beside ourselves. We went out to
see our friends, our relatives to relate to them
the strange, wonderful and miraculous event.
The Virgin from heaven concurred in sustain-
ing our imprudent faith and even the risky
steps which we took in the interest of her work.

Meanwhile here is what had transpired.

No sooner had the Countess and Miss Freda
left the Miccio home, than two young ladies,
Elisa Scotti and Giulia Torino began to recite
the fifteen mysteries of the Rosary; and two
souls from that very moment obtained new
life. From that instant the convulsions ceased;

and despite the darkest forebodings of a sure return of the same, they did not again renew themselves, in fact a most rapid recovery instantly set in.

On the 15th of that month, on Holy Saturday, Madam Concetta Miccio Vastarella, in perfect health left her house to make her Easter calls on her relatives, as is the custom; and first of all she visited her mother, who on seeing her could not cease to shed tears of joy.

All with one accord declared that that miraculous recovery was due to the promise made to the Virgin in regard to the *new church of the Rosary in Pompei.*

But it was not a single grace bestowed; but rather two.

The Virgin of the Rosary, who so early wished to give clear proof in Naples of her great satisfaction as regards the erection of a church in honor of her Rosary in Pompei, before yet the spot was known on which it would rise, and perhaps also to give us courage and strength to proceed in the arduous undertaking, saved two lives at the same time, that of the Mother and that of the child [1].

---

1) This beautiful proof of the mercy of the Most Blessed Virgin was proclaimed from the pulpit by tho elequent

A short while after Signor Giovanni Vastarella came himself in person to felicitate us
on the happy result; and the Countess returned to visit that family restored to happiness,
and now devoted to the work of the Temple
which was to be built in Pompei. And at the
same time, before the lenten season was over,
the same Signor Vastarella had the miracle
announced in the parochial church of Monte
Santo, and full of gratitude as he was, he offered me his services for the work of the
church, asking me to call on him for any and
every thing in which he could be of use. Together with his family and his newly resusci-
tated daughter he followed me to my dear little

Father Raphael Cocoz of the Order of Preachers, in the
Church of the Sapienza as well as in the Church of the
Rosary at Porta Medina in that same year 1876. And the
document signed by the witnesses was published in the
Journal " Lilies to Mary, „ Number of June 15, 1876.

Witnesses who signed: — Giovanni Vastarella — Luisa
Passaro — Vincenzo Miccio — Lawyer Vincenzo Vastarella -- Michele Cammarota Vastarella — Clorinda Lon-
ghi — Luigi Provino — Filippo Cammarota — Emilia Passaro — Cristina Matarese — Annina Vastarella — Gennaro
Passaro -- Elisetta Scotti — Giulia Torino — Gaetano
Passaro.

The document is signed by the doctor Professor Raphael Novi.

church of the Rosary at Porta Medina, and at the same Altar where I had declared myself son of the Third Order of the Rosary, they all took upon themselves the same habit, and so we became doubly brothers.

Thus the merciful Queen of the heavenly roses sweetened the first trials and tribulations of her servants with the ineffable comforts of her miracles.

And to day after a lapse of fourteen years since that event, we have seen the whole Miccio and Vastarella families, comprising the Signora Concetta, who yet remembers with a feeling of the most lively gratitude. how she was restored to life and health by the Virgin of Pompei, return to the feet of this miraculous Queen, here in the Valley of her predilection.

CHAPTER XI.

The Day set by God.

The extraordinary occurrence that had transpired in the Miccio-Vastarella household soon
ran from mouth to mouth throughout the
District of Saint Theresa and of Capodimonte
and the quarter of Montesanto; the impression it created was intense. The Virgin em-
ployed this means to predispose the hearts of
the good Neapolitans in favor of her work.

In my heart and in that of the Countess
there was an actual fever of excitement burning: we thought of nothing all day long but
the Church of Pompei: we spoke of nothing
else than of the ways and means to push the
work ahead with the same alacrity with
which it had been begun. — Our Lady — said
we — wants the church, and to this purpose
she performs miracles; therefore no human or
diabolical power can stand in its way.

But how raise the sacred walls without the
ground on which to build? Here we were always brought straight up against the same old
obstacle. We again turned to our ecclesiastical

Superior for counsel, so that he might show
us what path to choose in the name of God.

The holy Prelate on hearing these new marvels and the wonderful manner in which the
divine bounty clearly manifested its wishes
regarding the erection of the new church,
could not check the flow of his tears. His
answer was brief and precise so that it untied
every knot.

— After the many attempts made — said he —
to obtain a diminution of the price, nothing
remains to be done but to pay the price demanded by the proprietor. My advice is to buy
the land at any price and let it be that which
lies to the side of the Parish of the Most Holy
Saviour in the Province of Naples. —

The Pastor had spoken: there was no more
need of wavering or of discussing.

We again took up the propositions for the
purchase of the land; we acceeded to all the
pretensions of the lessee, of the holder and
of others and we fixed the day for the making
out of the necessary papers before the notary.

That day, preestablished by God and by Him
destined to open a series of so many and great
marvels, must have been a day of rejoicing
in Heaven. In that day we could foresee none

of the wonderful events which were to transpire, nor could human mind soar to the great-
ness of future portents.

This is God's usual way of conducting matters; He always acts when man least expects
Him to. Even His mercy reaches and touches
man when He is hoping for it the least. Each
and every one of us, if we only go back a little
and question our memory and our conscience
can bear witness to this fact. God came among
His creatures and His advent was silent and
unobserved. No one could have believed that
the Redeemer of humanity was already hidden
in that poor family which had come up from
Nazareth to sign its name on the roman regi-
ster, and was on that same night to appear to
the world.

Another mode of divine operation is silence:
God works in silence. The generation of the
Eternal Word takes place in silence. In silence
God descends into the bosom of a creature of
His and becomes the God-Man; and in perfect
silence does He perform the greatest miracle
of grace when He changes the heart of the
sinner into the heart of a saint; and in silence
Jesus performed His greatest wonder, argu-
ment of His divinity, His Resurrection. And

so too the greatest works to which man may lay his hand are conceived in silence. Noise is peculiar to man, who tries to help himself by a highsounding voice, by violent gesticulations and by great efforts, signs of his own impotence. So that the more man withdraws into silence, the closer he draws to God, the more easily he finds God.

Whoever had seen a few individuals in a room before a Notary Public sign an instrument of purchase of *twelve acres* of land, could never have foreseen to what a new era of mercy, shown to man from the abandoned waste of Pompei, that simple act was a forerunner.

Were it not that, as Faber remarks, all great and divine events when about to take place, so fill the spirit of man, that without his own knowledge, he becomes a prophet. And our spirit, inundated by a new and powerful joy, and filled with a burning thirst to see the Temple of the Lord soon built, feebly divined that something strange and unaccustomed was about to transpire. It ought to have been for us also a day of rejoicing and worthy of note, and such it was. On the 30th day of April 1876, day sacred to my beloved Saint Catherine of

Siena, the deed of purchase was signed by which we obtained the ground on which to build the House of the real God in the land of Pompei.

My sweet Saint did not forget this little sign of my love; three years later, as I will relate in this History, I received, by her intercession, a new lease of life.

———

CHAPTER XII.

The Archangel of Mount Gauro.

The deed was not yet signed when I proposed to the Bishop of Nola to fix the day for the solemn consecration and laying of the *cornerstone* of the Temple of Pompei.

— We must choose a feast-day, — remarked the venerable Prelate, — so that the farmers of the Valley can be present at the ceremony; and it appears to me that the first Sunday of next May which will be the seventh of the month, would be a suitable day.

— No, if you permit me — answered I; — for myself I should choose the eighth day of May, even though it does fall on a Monday, as it is the day sacred to the Archangel Saint Michael. And as that celestial Prince thrust Lucifer, the rebellious angel, out of Heaven's courts, so am I sure will he chase Satan from Valle di Pompei, where he has reigned for so many a century.

But this choice of a day sacred to the apparition of the Archangel of God, which I felt inspired to make for this first and great solemnity, forerunner of so many others, did not only arise from a feeling of deep devotion which I have for this noble Spirit of Heaven, but really from a higher reason.

Whosoever stands in this Valley and looks toward the south, naturally rests his eyes on the mountains that form an immense barrier to the south of Castellammare, of Gragnano and of Lettere. But one mountain among all, the others attracts his especial attention, first because more majestic than the others, almost like a giant custodian of the valley, and secondly because its summit is divided into three peaks, which present the shape of the thumb and first two fingers of our hand. And the third peak which is the highest, rises to heaven and again branches out into three other points.

The very name of the mountain contains a mystery; it was anciently *Gauro*, which as some would explain it, meant *Gaudio,* that is joy, or better, as others would have it, *Aureo,* golden, mountain of gold. The faithful changed this name into that of Monte San-Angelo, Mount Holy Angel, in consequence of the following event, which the Church celebrates in the office of the feast of Saint Catello, on the 19th of January.

It was the seventh century of the Church. A Saint, St. Catello, was Bishop of Castellammare, who is now venerated on the Altars as protector of that city. That holy Bishop was wont often in the night to retire to the recesses of the mountain in company with the Abbot of Sorrento, who was then Saint Antonino, of the Order of Saint Benedict, there to pray together.

One night, while they were praying there, the Archangel Saint Michael appeared to the Bishop of Castellammare, and told him to build a church in his honor on the summit of that mountain, on the spot which he would indicate by the apparition of a flame.

And the flame appeared on the highest point of the three peaks of Mount Gauro.

After innumerable difficulties and adversities which he had to surmount, and after being insulted and falsely accused in Rome, so that he was even imprisoned, the Holy Bishop of Castellammare succeeded in accomplishing the work enjoined on him by Heaven [1]). And immediately there appeared on that high peak a fresh fountain of crystalline and salubrious

---

1) See lessons on the Office of Saint Catello on the day of his feast, January 19th

water, which first served in the works of the building, and then served to quench the thirst of the numerous pilgrims who every year in the month of September went to venerate the Archangel St. Michael on the spot of his apparition, in the Temple erected by St. Catello [1]).

When on my first coming to Valle di Pompei, I learned this beautiful story of the apparition of St. Michael on Mount Gauro, from the Rev. Gennaro Federico, I soon devined that the greatest Prince of Heaven had some divine purpose to fulfill in this Valley. But at that time I was in ignorance of the purpose. Only it seemed evident to me that Saint Michael was the natural protector of this spot, that he had honored with his apparition and with the signs of his patronage.

---

1) The temple and the pilgrimages lasted till 1860, when the brigands made a stronghold of it for themselves, and our soldiers, in order to oust the latter, destroyed the ancient monument. The Bishop of Castellammare saved the precious marble statue, representing the Archangel Saint Michael, which Saint Catello had brought twelve centuries before from Rome and placed there. And now His Excellency Mons. Sarnelli, present Bishop of Castellammare has placed this historical relic in a large and richly adorned Chapel built in the new Cathedral of that city, where it is greatly venerated.

For this reason, with my heart full of such sentiments, I did not hesitate to make my proposition to the Bishop of Nola, as I have already stated.

— Saint Michael the Archangel, — added I, addressing the worthy Prelate — was the Guardian Angel of the Blessed Virgin during her life on earth, St. Michael is the Patron of all the Temples of the living God, and St Michael shall be the Guardian and Protector of the Temple of Pompei. —

The Bishop of Nola, to please me, consented.

My presentiments were not wrong. The powerful and glorious Prince, always kind to us, has repeatedly allowed us to feel the beneficent effects of his protection. Innumerable have been the victories gained by Saint Michael on this spot over all enemies visible and invisible, both of ourselves and this Sanctuary. His apparition in the 7th Century indicated the preparation for the reign of Mary in this desolate, unknown and abandoned country, that had one day been under the rule of sin and Satan. The great Archangel came to chase Satan from the land of the gentiles, where a new era of grace was to begin, and a new Sun of mercy to rise.

However matters may stand, this much is certain, that inspired by the reading of this apparition, we proposed to the Bishop of Nola in 1876 that the day on which the cornerstone of this Sanctuary of Mary was to be laid should be the *8th day of May,* because sacred to the glory of that Angel who was the Guardian of Mary on earth and is the Defender of all the Sanctuaries of Mary throughout the world; and who, having appeared in this Valley, should by good reason be its singular protector.

And now during the course of seventeen years, we have always, on that 8th day of May, called with faith upon the first Angel of Heaven to celebrate together with us the glories of our common Queen. And in each year we celebrate two solemn epiphanies. The greatest Prince of Heaven, whose name is glorious, manifested himself to earth, choosing as a scene of his wonders the peak of a mountain. The greatest Queen that heaven and earth have ever had, has manifested herself to the sorrowing sons of Eve, choosing as centre of her marvels the *humble Valley* of a buried city.

But the Virgin, wishing to still further

strengthen our faith in her protection and give new vigor to our reliance on her, so that the future battles, which we were to encounter, should not discourage us, or turn us from our undertaking, wished to perform still another miracle, a fifth one, before our laying the foundation stone.

CHAPTER XIII.

A fifth sign from Heaven before laying the Cornerstone of the Sanctuary.

The Rev. Anthony Varone, 56 years of age, and residing in Naples in the Vico Paradiso alla Salute, N° 65, toward the middle of April of that same year was attacked by malignant typhus, complicated with erysipelas and internal and external cancrene; which latter extending down from his knees to his toes, and hideously deforming his hands, his face, his whole mouth and even his tongue, made him an unpleasant sight to look on. And so going from bad to worse, on the 23ʳᵈ of April, at the end of his strength and despaired of by the Doctors, he took the last Sacraments. The attending physician, Doctor Vincenzo Marsilia, continually drew from his mouth strata of cancrene, and during his absence the assisting friends did likewise.

A consultation was held with the Professors Raphael Valieri and Clemente del Gaudio, and all declared « that nothing more was to be hoped for from human art: that divine power alone could save him from inevitable

death ». Various persons present at the consultation were auricular witnesses to these
words.

All the inhabitants of the immediate neigh-
borhood and of the entire city district of the
Salute were very sorrowful at the thought of
the imminent loss of this priest beloved by
all who knew him, and all inquired with the
greatest anxiety from their windows and along
the street for news whenever the doctor passed. Don Federico Caprioli, hearing of the
many miraculous favors obtained in Naples
through offerings made to the new Church in
Pompei, still felt a hope; and that very day,
which was a Sunday, he begged the Countess
to go to the house of the dying man and obtain
from him a vow in case of his recovery.

The Countess enters the house and finds it
full of weeping persons she did not know; among
them were the Messrs. Vincenzo Barone, Errico Sorrentino, Vincenzo Marzano, the priest
Vincenzo Varriale, the Rev. Raphael Guglielmi,
the Rev. Pasquale Barone, Joseph Lebano, and
many others who were expecting every moment the now inevitable death of their friend.
The Countess approached the bedside of the
dying man, who with his face hideously swol-

len, half purple, half black, his mouth open,
his lips black and turgid, his breast heaving,
appeared to be breathing his last. At such a
sight a certain shudder of horror ran through
her, but overcoming her feelings she said:
— Father, the Virgin of the Rosary of Pompei
is performing miracles for her new Church.
Will you promise me to publish the fact to
all people and to leave a written document
if you obtain your recovery? —

At these words the patient wept and with
difficulty answered: — I will fulfill everything
you promise in my name. And he joined his
hands as though in prayer while all the by-
standers on their knees recited a Hail Mary
to the Virgin of the Rosary of Pompei. All
were weeping and the Countess added: — Have
faith, Our Lady will grant you your request. —

The evening of that very Sunday, lo, recovery
set in, the cancrene began to detach itself and
the body, the face and the mouth to be covered
with new skin, and even the fingers began to
grow new nails.

Restored to health and thinking all to have
been a dream, even the visit of a lady who
had spoken to him of some church to be built
in Pompei, he thought to fully satisfy his de-

votional duty by celebrating a thanksgiving
Mass in the Church of Saint Nicholas Tolentino, where there is a Virgin of Lourdes greatly
venerated, and thus reasoned with himself:
— It is all the same, Lourdes or Pompei, the
Virgin is the same. And I will save myself a
trip to Pompei.

But the Queen of the world, who for some
high purpose has chosen this spot to be particularly honored in preference to so many
others and wants her children to come here
to pray to her, allowed, what we will now relate, to happen.

It was the 12th day of June, and the Countess
together with ourselves, having been informed
of the priest's recovery, went to seé him in
order to obtain the promised document and
such offerings as he had been able to collect
from the faithful. But to our great surprise
we first learned, and afterward saw with our
own eyes, that the priest was again a-bed, tormented by a raging fever and severe pains.

Surprised and sorrowful we asked the cause
of this new illness, but no one could give any
reason.

We asked him what he had done for the
church of Pompei and learning that he had

given the matter no thought, we did not hesitate to remind him of his promises and begged him to carry them out so as to regain his
health.

He then promised to publicly announce the
miracle and to go to Pompei and relate it to
the Bishop and all persons there.

And that night, when it was feared he would
grow worse, he suddenly became perfectly well
so that in the morning he arose and left his
house to celebrate Mass.

On the day of the Feast of the Rosary the
Rev. Antonio Varone was in Valle di Pompei;
he celebrated Mass, and during the celebration, with tears streaming from his eyes, he
told to all the wonderful event [1]).

---

1) This fact was corroborated by the undersigned witnesses: Rev. Antonio Varone, — Rev. Frederic Caprioli —
Countess Marianna De Fusco — Vincenzo Marzano — Francis Anselmi — Rev. Gennaro Gattone — Gaetano Nigro —
Rev. Pasquale Parone — Fathei Basilio of Naples — Amato
Nigro — Antonio Nigro — Vincenzo Barone — Errico Sorrentino — Vincenzo Sorrentino — Louis Vecchione — Josephine Salvati — Rev. Vincenzo Varriale — Joseph Lebano — Gennaro Pellizzone — Rev. Raphael Guglielmi —
Bartolo Longo Esq. — There are besides the attestations
of Doctor Vincenzo Marsilia and of Professor Raphael
Valieri.

CHAPTER XIV.

The 8th of May 1876 — The Corner Stone of the Sanctuary.

And the much longed for and much contested day arrived, the day sacred to the Prince of the Angels, the 8th of May; and it fell in that year, as we have already said, on a Monday.

We raised a tent on the ground recently purchased and covered with grass and furrows; and beneath this tent, on two barrels on which rested a plank covered with a cloth and hangings, we formed a table and an altar.

A crucifix and six candles, this was the gorgeous array which was to serve at the beginning of the foundation of the Temple of Pompei, which was so shortly to become monumental, of world-wide fame!... At the back of the tent, above the high part of the altar, in a gilded frame, was hung the Old Image of the Rosary, not yet retouched by Maldarelli, but still as it had been restored by the first painter, who was Signor Galella as we have already stated.

The Bishop of Nola, in whose diocese lies Pompei, accompanied by his Vicar, by Canons

and by the Curate of Nola, and by other priests
from various parts, came in solemn pomp to
this Valley for the touching ceremony of laying the cornerstone of the Temple of God.

It was an enchanting day; the sky was serene, without a cloud: out in the open country,
fragrant with sweet field flowers and brilliant
in its dress of green, opposite Mount Vesuvius, that majestically raised its crest of smoke, and near the amphitheatre, which at that
time was not yet hidden from the traveller's
view by the earth works with which it is to-
day surrounded, the most beautiful and tender
rites of the catholic church were performed,
by means of which this abandoned spot was
soon to be changed into the *holy habitation
of God,* and this desert land into a *Sanctuary,*
into a *Road to Heaven.*

The witnesses to such solemn rites were only
poor peasants and a little crowd of about
three hundred neapolitan ladies and gentlemen, among whom several had received favors.

Among others were to be seen the families
of the Messrs. Miccio and Vastarella together with Madam Concetta restored to life by
the Madonna of Pompei. There was also the

family of Madam Anna Maria Lucarelli of Naples, who bore witness to the *first miracle* granted by Heaven at the intercession of the Most Blessed Virgin invoked by the totally new title *of Pompei*. There was present Joseph Federico already mentioned, and all his children who were fulfilling their promise; Ernestina Freda, the Duchess of Messanella, the Marchioness Ruffo with her family, and the Messrs. Murena and Lavorgna of Naples surrounded us.

Oh how dear to all who were so happy as to come here on that 8th of May 1876 is the memory of that day!

Who can think how great a glory it be to God and men to build a Temple on the ancient land of Pompei dedicated to the Virgin Mary? But who can adequately appreciate the immense advantages which shall accrue to all these inhabitants for the course of future centuries from this new church of Valle di Pompei?

No doubt a great crown of merit awaits in the next world all those generous souls of the faithful who with catholic charity have brought their offerings here.

Strange coincidence of human events! To the foolish and the incredulous, who cannot

understand the ultimate scope and reason of
certain facts, such matters appear to be but
simple chance; but to the believer, in the light
of the philosophy of history, the perennial
law of order and of divine Providence will
be manifest, that so admirably rules over and
ordains all human events! On that same day,
at that same hour, by an unforeseen coincidence, a huge man-of-war, the Duilio, is launched into the waters of Castellammare di
Stabia. And that, at a distance of four miles;
in the Valle di Pompei, another mystical *Ship*
is begun, and baptized with the more glorious
and triumphant title of the *Queen of the Rosary.*

Yonder, over that product of earthly strength
and glory, a Prince of the world presides [1])
here, in his humility and at the same time his
majesty, over a work of love only and divine
glory, presides a Pastor of Holy Church, the
Bishop of Nola; who invested with the authority which comes to him from Christ, changes
the cold marble into a holy thing, and with
it lays his hand to the edifice which unites
in sacred bonds of love Heaven and Earth,
God and Man, Time and Eternity.

---

1) King Victor Emmanuel the 2 nd

Again, that formidable vessel, iron-clad, is intended as an instrument of *death*. This holy *Vessel,* work of love and of peace, will be the means of giving eternal *life* to many sinners, who will here be cleansed in the fountain of Penance; to many afflicted mothers and widowed wives, who will here obtain eternal peace for the souls of their beloved departed; to many sick and languishing, afflicted and dying, who will here find the life-giving balsam for their wounds, relief for their anguish, help in all their trials, and the return of ebbing life.

In Castellammare, an immense crowd of people from every part, great movement, and bustle, great confusion by land and sea, banners and decorations, joyful applause and the happy strains of music, flowers and light, gay apparel and display of fleeting beauty; in Valle di Pompei poor peasants and simple women, crowds of bright and active children, and people of a ripe old age [1]) on whose face

---

1) Here in Valle di Pompei there are many cases of long life. That day an old man was present 107 years old; his name was Joseph Zeppetella, and his wife was 105 years old. Shortly after the husband died, and fifteen days later the wife. To-day an old peasant, by

shines the pure joy of the soul, and an affectionate and tranquil piety. No other sounds
but the lively ringing of two small bells, which
from time to time with their gay peals announce a religious festival to the surrounding
valleys. No cry of enthusiasm no noise of any
sort, but the sweet and mournful silence of
the verdant fields, interrupted only by the
placid and fervent prayers of the faithful, who,
moved even to tears, unite their voices to
the eternal chants of the Angels, who certainly glorified God in this spot destined to

---

name Catello, has come to bring us his good wishes,
and he carries very well on his shoulders the weight
of 106 years. And the guardian of the Via Sacra, Angelo
Solimene, one of the great-grandfathers of the present
generation of Valle, whose duty it is with his spade to
repair any damage done to the road by horses and car-
riages, is 92 years of age and still works. During the
course of 19 years that we have been working in this
spot not one of those who began the church with us
has died, save the old Parish Priest Cirillo, who was
the *first Pastor* of the modern Valle, and whose age was
79 years; and the evening before his death he had come
to the Parish to give the evening Benediction. Joseph
Federico was 75, and Angelo Tortora, the teamster who
brought the Image of the Rosary to the Valley on his
dung-laden cart, was also 75, and Ferdinand Vitiello
was 89 years old!

become *His Sanctuary, His abode, the Throne of His mercies.*

The learned, holy and inspired prayer recited with intense fervor by that distinguished orator, Paolino Antiello, canonical curate of Marigliano, so moved the hearts of all present, that they offered on the spot more than 100 francs towards the new building. A gentleman presented a cross of gold, and a poor young girl having nought else to give, generously took off her earrings and laid them down to help building the house of the Madonna.

It was eleven o' clock in the morning, and the Bishop was blessing the corner-stone, the air was tranquil, not a breeze blew, all was wrapt in a religious silence. When suddenly, while cutting with the point of the knife the sign of the holy cross on the marble, there was heard a creaking of branches, a murmur of wind which blowing about the bushes, and growing stronger and stronger like a small whirlwind, soon enveloped all in a dense cloud of dust. It was as though all nature felt the power of the cross of Christ.

Shortly after we all, who had been prostrate on the ground, arose and forming a sacred procession, we followed the good Bishop of

16

Nola, who surrounded by the levites went to place in its cavity the *first stone* of the Sanctuary of Mary, intoning the Litany of the Saints.

At that very moment the boom of the cannon was heard, which saluting the earthly king in Castellamare and resounding through the Valle di Pompei, seemed with its deep voice to venerate the accomplishment of so celestial a ceremony, and to salute in its language that *Corner-Stone,* on which was to be built the Church of God.

Thus on this desolate land was planted the banner of the Cross, emblem of blessing, of civilization and of redemption.

In the cavity dug for the first fundamental pilaster of the Temple, which is the first pillar of the great arch to the left, beneath the *first stone* of the divine edifice, we placed some gold, silver and bronze coins, acknowledging thus the supreme dominion that God has over Earth as well as Heaven, over us and our belongings. In the same brass casket containing the coins, we placed in a glass tube our written name, that of the Countess, and of the Rev. Federico and of others who in those early times gave us valid help. It was an expression of filial confidence in the patronage of the Mother of God. It was a symbol of faith in Christ our King, Master, Redeemer and Judge, beneath whose aegis we wanderers combat, and in Whose omnipotent name we will be crowned victors.

To-day, whosoever enters the Sanctuary of Pompei, and looks to the left where the large aisle ends, at the base of the pilaster supporting the cupola, can read this inscription, that recalls that day and solemn ceremony and indicates the spot where the corner-stone of the Temple was laid:

ON THE EIGHTH DAY OF MAY MDCCCLXXVI
BY JOSEPH FORMISANO BISHOP OF NOLA,
IN THE PRESENCE OF THE FOUNDERS
BARTOLO LONGO ESQ. AND WIFE, COUNTESS MARIANNA DE FUSC)
AND A COTERIE OF CITIZENS AND PATRICIANS OF NAPLES
THE CORNER STONE OF THE SANCTUARY WAS HERE LAID
FOR THE USE OF POOR PEASANTS,
WHICH CEASELESS FAVORS AND MIRACLES
HAVE MADE TO REACH ITS PRESENT SPLENDOR.

Not far from the Amphitheatre of Pompei, belonging to the city once so gay with gentile amusements and polluted with the worship of idols and of demons, and now made mute and desert in ruin and devastation, there rose finally, on the day sacred to the

Prince of Angels, silent but sublime the Cross of the Christ-God, ever bearer of life and true civilization to all nations and people. There the tired wanderèr and weary peasant will sometimes rest beneath the shadow of the Altar dedicated to the Virgin Mother, who with the Infant Saviour on her arms, and the Rosary in her right hand, shows them *the old remedy for all ills, the destruction of heresies, the Help of Chistians.*

She from this new throne of mercy, holding in her hand the emblem of her love and dolours, namely the rosary and the cross, turns to mortals and says:

— Oh, all of you who are wearied and oppressed by sorrow, take the remedy for your wounds. Here is my crown of heavenly Roses; gird your heart with it: offer it up every day at my feet and I will save you from death. Your life on earth is an exile, a pilgrimage; you arc dust; but my Roses cannot fade and are lifegiving. And I, who am the Mother of sinners, will come to crown you in the day of your agony.

. .

Now the formidable iron-clad, the Duilio, is launched to fulfill its destiny: and this mystical Ship is nearing its completion, and needs those who shall complete it. For the former, a thing wholly material and perishable, exposed to a thousand perils, millions of francs were spent, for this, a work wholly celestial and spiritual, and infinitely superior and more beneficent, a subscription of only a *cent a month* has been asked! But the Virgin Mary is omnipotent by grace. More than two millions and a half francs have already been spent on this Temple!...

Mary, who in these days wishes to save souls with that same Rosary with which she saved civil society in the XIII century, and which She herself recited there on the mountain of Lourdes; our sweet and merciful Mother wishes this Temple to be named after her and after the symbol of her love for men, the *Rosary*. And the extraordinary events that have taken place during these last twenty years, and the favors She grants to the faithful of every class, and of every nation, so only they help in the building of her Temple so dear to Her, give ample security of this and open the heart to the sweetest hopes.

BOOK FOURTH
The foundations of the Temple.

CHAPTER I.

May 1876.

§ 1.

THE DESIGN OF THE SANCTUARY.

The cornerstone of the building, that was one day to become the *House of the Lord* in the desert land of Pompei, had been solemnly laid, and in the great and glowing desires of our heart, it seemed to us as though we had overcome all the great difficulties that had arisen since the very first hour of the undertaking, and had at last reached the ardently longed for day when we were to lay the foundations of a Temple to the living God on the land of pagan divinities.

But the festivities over and cold reason hav-

ing claimed its rights, we began to foresee
greater and more numerous difficulties than
any we had encountered before.

And in the first place how large was this
new church to be? How broad, how long?
How many altars and chapels was it to contain?

Evangelical prudence counseled not to undertake anything over and above our strength.
A warning of the holy Bishop of Nola was in
every wise similar:

— Do not spend any more than you hold. —

On the other hand however we well remembered another wise saying of that worthy
Prelate, and which was the fruit of his long
experience: — When a church is to be built
from the very foundations, it is not the present
number of inhabitants of a place that one
must consider, but the increasing number they
will amount to twenty years thence. —

In view of these words foresight would
counsel the building of a church ample enough
to accommodate two-thousand persons, calculating at ten-fold the increase of the population in twenty years.

But how conciliate the two contrary dic-
tums? Monsignor Formisano himself had found

this simple solution.—Do not lay your foundations all at once but little by little, according to the amonnt of money you hold. Then you can begin to raise two walls on these pieces of foundation, later on an arch, then a vault; between the two lateral walls temporarily raise a third one to close them, and behold a little church built and ready. In the year following you can throw down the temporary wall and continue to build your foundations, and then the walls together with arches and another vault, and behold the problem as to the length of the church resolved. Thus from year to year by tearing down the temporary wall and raising the permanent walls, you can lengthen your church to your heart's desire.

Wholly ignorant as we were of the science of architecture this proposal seemed most wise, as it appeared to conciliate the counsels of *prudence* with those of *foresight*.

But there was still another problem to be solved.

How were these foundations to be built? Were they to be one solid mass of concrete, or were they for economy's sake to consist in arches and pilasters? And supposing the

question of economy was to be considered
how broad were these arches and these pilasters to be?

And again what form of a church, if a church
was to be built, would be most fitted to contain
a future, hypothetical, population of two thous-
and peasants, or in other words which style
was to be chosen? Columns or pilasters, one
nave or three, latin or greek cross? A vault
of masonry, or a ceiling of woodwork and a
roof of tiles? All these problems were for me
of difficult solution.

To make a long story short, some kind of
an architectural drawing was necessary before any work could be undertaken.

But have recourse to an architect? Heaven
forefend! Marchioness Filiasi and Monsignor
Formisano had warned us sufficiently against
calling on the services of an architect for a
rustic church for poor peasants, when it would
have required more than half the sum collected
with so much difficulty merely to pay the
former's fees and traveling expenses. Better
than pay out money to an architect would it
be, so reasoned we, to employ the sum in the
building. This had become a kind of conviction
with me.

Yet nevertheless a drawing was absolutely necessary. What was to be done?

Obedient as ever to the words of the Pastor, we decided to follow his counsels, and to build piecemeal. In this wise we could circumvent for the present the first difficulty which was to decide upon the length of the church. But how broad was it to be? I could not leave the width undetermined or else how could the lateral excavations be begun?

I did not loose my courage. The acme of all my designs was to build a church to the living God in this forsaken spot, and to lead this new born population to invoke the Queen of Victories to their aid with the precious chaplet of the *Rosary*. The result would be the same whatever the style or shape of the church. Hence it was unnecessary to worry over that matter. Four whitewashed walls were all that was necessary, and a simple whitewashed vault; and the country folk could enter in and worship God.

Beside which I had another thought in my mind. I had seen near Scafati a church quite spacious enough, capable of holding more than a thousand persons, dedicated to Our Lady, with a single nave, in the shape of a latin cross, whose whitewashed walls lent it an air of joyfulness and purity. Oh how happy would I have deemed myself to have seen a similar church in my Valle di Pompei! I immediately asked for information, and was told that it had been *thirty years* in building and had cost nothing less than *thirty thousand* francs!....

Thirty years of labor! *thirty thousand* francs down! That was enough to frighten one at the very outset. And who could collect such a sum among the poor peasants of Valle di Pompei? And who was to assure me, so feeble of health, that I would live that number of years?

— Do not be selfish, — our Bishop had ofttimes repeated: — do not think of yourselves but of posterity. You begin, others will finish. —

These words rang constantly in our hearts. We were to begin, without dreaming of beholding the completion. Therefore faith in the aid of Providence, and to work! *We will begin, others will finish!* Let the church of Our Lady in Scafati be the model even if the future church of Pompei was to be a very humble copy!

Having come to this decision, and not knowing what else better to do, we invited our master mason, Pasquale Vitiello, to accompany us to the church at Scafati. And one fine day, together with the Countess and a priest who was a friend of ours, we betook ourselves thither, and with a roll of twine we took all the measurements as to lenght and breadth. And having discovered that Don Gennaro had a natural bent for mechanics, I requested him to make me a drawing of a church similar to the one we were measuring. He without loss of time made me a drawing on a piece of paper of an edifice purporting to be a church, with a single nave and four chapels.

To be perfectly frank that drawing must have been very grotesque, as having shown it to several professional architects it aroused the greatest hilarity. But to us, brimming over with impatience, and sorry to loose even an hour, it appeared more than sufficient to begin work on.

Don Gennaro proposed beside, in order to economize, not to pay the laborers by the job but by the day, and added that he and his father, who had promised to lend his gratuitous aid, would themselves superintend the work and see that all matters proceeded regularly.

And we also resolved, still having an eye to economy, that the foundations should be made with vaults and pilasters.

§ 2.

THE FIRST STONES CARRIED ON MEN'S SHOULDERS

In order to carry on the work with as little expense and at the same time as rapidly as possible, the old Pastor of Valle di Pompei, whom we have already presented to our readers, decided to invite on the following Sunday all the farmers and teamsters of the valley to offer some their labor on holidays, others a cartload of stones, others still a little mortar or any other building material.

Not more than five hundred yards from the spot where the church was to rise, a small quarry of volcanic stones had been opened by one of the Custodians of the Excavations of Pompei, Pietro Paolo Vitiello by name, who had at his own expense and in order to build himself a house, already prepared a certain provision of those stones. And when he witnessed the ceremony of the laying of the corner-stone of the new church he decided within his heart to offer to this holy Work twelve cubic metres of stones, and merely awaited the carts to transport them.

On the Sunday following the 8th day of May, having gathered together all the population of the valley, the reverend Pastor rose to preach and thus addressed the congregation: « God, my children, has taken pity on you, and has disposed that a church rise in your midst where you can worthily congregate and become good Christians. It is most meritorious in man to build a church to the living God, and hence every one of you should feel honored to help as far as in him lies toward the building of a house wherein is to dwell the Most High. And as the Custodian of ancient Pompei has offered to furnish a certain quantity of stones it would be a most meritorious work of penance and of piety if you were to transport these stones on your own shoulders, as a symbol of your subjection to the God of heaven and earth ».

The words of the priest fell like good seed on fertile ground. Every single person there, men and women, young and old, followed the desires and example of their Pastor.

The venerable Curate took the lead, and behind him followed, as though in a procession, the two priestly Federico brothers, then the Countess with her four children, all the servants of the household and all her farmers, and the mingled crowd of the inhabitants of the valley, boys and girls comprised. It was indeed a touching sight to behold so many persons of all ages returning along the provincial highway that from Naples leads to Salerno, all bowed beneath the weight of stones that with humble and sincere faith they carried on their shoulders, regardless of all human prejudices.

I too was among the number of those fortunate ones, and carried my stone on my shoulder; and perchance that noble humiliation has borne me the fruit of having the infinite joy to behold the house of the Lord almost completed.

The Countess and her daughter Joan also carried their stone, and twelve years later the latter was to owe her life to that very church a stone toward the building of which she had carried on her arms.

The first born son, Count Francesco De Fusco, had the same honor, and he too, fifteen years later, through prayers offered up in that very church returned from death unto life. Oh how bountifully God rewards even in this life those who serve Him, and with what a paternal eye does He looks upon all who help to raise temples and altars to His Name!

Each and every one of us in that moment was animated by an inexpressible faith: our minds could most certainly not foresee the future destinies of that rustic church, about to be erected for poor peasant-folk. No! but the all absorbing thought was, *to have God adored in this spot where He was so little known,* and to render unto Him those acts of homage, love, and adoration which every creature owes to his Creator.

Oh! how one's heart exults to-day at the memöry of any act of humility and penance one was led, by God's grace, to perform on that day of mercies! To think that we, with our own hands, placed a stone in the foundations of a temple to the Lord; and of what a temple! of a temple that only eighteen years afterwards was to be declared, by the visible Head of Christianity, a Pontifical Sanctuary!...

If on that Sunday, the 14ᵗʰ day of May, 1876, some sceptic had beheld a certain person on the country highway from Naples to Salerno, with heaving chest, and wet with perspi-

ration because of the burning rays of the
May sun, stopping from time to time to
take breath, and to deposit the heavy stone
he carried, on the parapet at the side of
the road; then again to lift the weight, and
hurry forward as though impelled by some
unseen force, that septic would undoubtedly
have mocked and derided him: while he, at
that time, absorbed by one sole feeling, that
of *faith,* would most probably have disregar-
ded the insult. To-day, nineteen years from that
date, after the numberless signs of mercy
shewn from the temple of Pompei to the
world, one would lay down one's burden by
the way-side, and with gentle force, lent by
love of Our Lady, draw the scoffer here to the
feet of her, Our Mother, *to behold the wonders
of the Lord in the land of Gentiles.* The serene
and kindly glance of Our Queen would not
suffer him to depart without a blessing! And
the blessing of Mary is ever the harbinger of
faith and of peace, even when it appears to
bestow therewith a martyrdom. Blessed indeed is he who loves and honours so gentle,
so sweet a Queen!

§ 3.

FALSE BEGINNINGS
AND THEIR LAMENTABLE CONSEQUENCES.

Thus the first pile of stones was made, with which to begin the foundations of the Church of Pompei. And the example of the zealous Custodian was followed by proprietors of stone-quarries, by lime vendors, and by teamsters; so that nothing more was lacking, and digging could be begun: the hand was laid to the spade, and the ground was broken.

But in order to present to our readers a clearer idea of the difficulties we had to encounter, it will not be out of place for us to give a description of the volcanic nature of the land that was to receive the foundations. In this portion of the valley it is in layers, and the upper soil is not deeper than a yard; indeed in some parts less. This is formed by ashes from Vesuvius, thrown out in the years following the great eruption of 79; it has been rendered most fertile by the constant industry of the peasants, assisted by frequent irrigations due to the canal of the river Sarno; so that this warm soil, refreshed by copious streams,

readily yields the patient cultivator four har
vests a year.

But beneath this very fertile layer there lies
another, hard and sterile, formed of ashes and
iron kneaded together with the boiling water
ejected from Vesuvius in the famous year 79.

It is in this subsoil that the modern Pompeians are accustomed to lay the foundations
of their houses.

Beneath this *tasso*, as the geologists call
it, lies buried a stratum of *lapilli*, small white
stones, light and porous as sponges, and that
nevertheless sufficed to bury a vast city entirely; such was the quantity that rained from
the fiery mountain, destroying the pagan abode
of luxury and profligacy.

This layer of *lapilli* is from three to four
yards deep, and is from time to time inter-
spersed with others of *tasso*, about half a yard
deep.

This deep stratum of *lapilli* rests on the soil
once cultivated by the ancient Pompeians,
and which is reddish and fertile. Various
objects of interest have been discovered in
this sub-stratum of earth near Pompei, coins,
skeletons of birds, and the skeleton of a slave,
to judge from the chains on his ankles. From the

state in which the soil was found, it was easy
to infer the mode of cultivation of the ancient
Pompeians, who divided the ground in broad
strips, intersecting them with little canals,
such as can be seen to this day in the swampy
lands near Naples.

Beneath the *lapilli,* sometimes in the middle
of them, are to be found veins of water, in
some parts most fresh and drinkable, in others
iron and magnesia abound in excess.

And now having given an idea of the Geo-
logical formation in these parts, let us return
to our history.

Joseph Federico, who was an enterprising
man and experienced in business matters,
having observed that the master-masons of
Scafati demanded higher pay than those of
Boscotrecase, a master-mason of that town,
Luigi Cirillo by name, was called in, to com-
mence the foundations of the new Church.

But Cirillo, not thinking of the weight that
these would be called upon to bear, sunk
them only two and a half yards deep in the
second layer of tasso, before described.

Being quite uncertain as to whether or not
we were doing the right thing, with regard
to the building, we felt absolutely obliged to

consult an architect, and the Countess knowing an old engineer in Naples, Sig. Francesco Aratore, a most pious man, architect of the new home, Miss Catherine Volpicelli had had built for the Sisters of the Sacred Heart, we one evening went to call on him.

As soon as he heard of our manner of proceeding he greatly marvelled at our not having consulted a competent authority on the subject.

We besought him to come to Valle di Pompei for a day at least, and to examine the freshly opened foundations. But he excused himself, alleging his old age and infirmities, but offering to send in his stead his young assistant.

Two days afterwards the latter came to Pompei to look at the excavations already begun.

It is needless to say that he completely disapproved of all that had been done. « Your foundation pilasters » he remarked, « if you wish them to be solid and firm must be settled below the water ». It was therefore necessary to undo what had already been begun, and to dig down still further, and to place the vaults underground so as to render them immovable.

For a church destined to contain two thousand people, the pilasters were weak, and the arches too superficial. Time at least, if not money, had been wholly wasted; this was a sore trial for our hearts; and, as is usual with every one whose peace of mind is disturbed, we began to consider to whom we could turn to unburden our cares and anxieties.

It seemed to us that no one could better comfort us than the Bishop of Nola; to him therefore we immediately sent the priest Don Gennaro to inform him minutely of all that had occurred.

The good Bishop, at first, was taken sadly by surprise, and not knowing what course to choose he remarked:

« Suspend all work till I send you *Master Salvatóre*. He will decide what is to be done and then I will come in person to Valle di Pompei ».

§ 4.

DISAPPOINTMENT.

Salvatore Taddeo was a mason of Nola, nearer seventy than sixty years of age, a man of integrity and experience in his trade therefore Monsignor Formisano had had re-

course to his services in restoring part of
the Seminary; and such was the esteem in
which he held him, that the worthy Prelate
never began any building without first having
recourse to his old and trusted mason. On the
other hand such was the veneration Taddeo
felt for the old Bishop, that he never dissented
a jot or tittle from the latter's opinions.

On the day fixed we all gathered together
on the brink of the excavations, the Countess and myself, the Federico family, father and sons, the master-mason of Boscotrecase, Luigi Cirillo, and *Master Salvatore,*
as chief oracle.

It may please the reader to hear the conversation held on this occasion, as it will go
to prove still further how the Sanctuary of
Pompei, had it been the work of man alone,
would still to this day not have risen above
its foundations!

— What say you, Master Salvatore, are these
foundations well laid? I asked.

— Oh, yes! quite well! —

— But the assistant of the architect Signor
Aratore, has observed that they are superficial,
and hence should be relaid. —

— Well, yes! they are superficial!

— But are you of opinion that by laying the pillars deeper, we should be more sure to build well ? —

— Oh , yes ! perhaps it would be better to do so.

— But is not the fear of our Bishop well founded, namely, that an eruption of Vesuvius could cause the building to collapse with such foundations?

— Yes , there is a danger that Vesuvius might be the cause of a catastrophe.

— Then would it not be wiser to lay the foundations in concrete? in that case would an eruption be destructive to the building?

— No, then there would be no fear of danger.

— How are we to decide upon the length and width of the concrete foundation? His Lordship has told us to build by piecemeal; two walls now, and next year to add to them, and so on year by year, as Providence sends us the money. What say you?

— That would be well too.

One was obliged to exercise much self control not to lose the little patience still remaining.

In order not to offend the old mason, I laughingly changed the subject, and making

a sign to my companions, turned away from
the broken-up ground and left for Naples,
most sadly disappointed at heart.

§. 5.

How Professor Antonio Cua of the University of Naples offered to gratuitously direct the building of the Sanctuary.

While I was thus sorely tried and embarrassed, God, Who was providentially guiding
the threads of His own work, drew me from
my perplexity in a most surprising manner.

I went to the house of the Cavalier Tarquinio Fuortes, an intimate friend of mine, and
Professor of mathematics in the military college of the Nunziatella; he, though young in
years, possessed much artistic taste and knowledge, and his noble and sincere character-
istics are to be greatly admired.

It is needless to say that he and all his family had been among our first associates in
the schemes connected with the future church
of Pompei.

The morning I went to call on him, I found
him surrounded by his family, and friends,

amongst them an elderly gentleman of venerable mien, wholly unknown to me.

Nothing could be more desirable to me
than to find strangers in the homes of my
friends, as I was thus offered the chance of finding new subscribers to the church of Pompei.
And so, preoccupied solely by my all absorbing thought, and without waiting for introductions, I began to relate to my friend all that had
recently happened to me in Valle di Pompei.

The stranger, after listening to me for a
while, interrupted me by saying,

— Pray, who is the architect who directs
your works?

— Oh! answered I, with a smile and, shaking
my head, — we have no architects.

— What! — exclaimed the gentleman, greatly
surprised — for the church you are building,
in laying the foundations, you have no architect to guide you? you have at least an
architectural design? —

— Oh! that yes — answered I.

— And pray who designed it?

— We ourselves.... that is to say, a young
friend of mine, a priest, who copied it from
a plan of a church near by. —

— I should like to see the drawing — remark-

ed the stranger, with a certain air of supe-
riority, as of a master toward a delinquent
scholar.

And I, who always carried my drawing with
me, ready at any moment to shew it, put
my hand in my pocket, and drew forth the
famous paper my readers already knows.

As soon as the gentleman beheld the drawing, a smile of compassion overspread his
features.

— But why — inquired he — in an undertaking
of this kind, not have recourse to a person
competent in the matter?

— Because the fees and expenses of an architect would absorb half the money collected
with so much difficulty.

— Oh! that is an exaggeration — answered
the stranger becoming serious. Moreover there
might be some architects who would lend
their services gratuitously.

— I would never accept the offer; I said in-
terruptingly, — the Bishop of Nola, Marchione
Filiasi and Father Ludovico of Casoria found
themselves in a heap of trouble on that very
account.

— We must distinguish facts, — gravely remarked the stranger, not all men are alike, nor

all cases either. Give me your drawing and
I will make it anew for you, according to the
rules of architecture.

I, who was intensely prejudiced, through
ignorance and inexperience, against all architects, and had not the slightest idea as to
who the gentleman was, felt quite taken aback
by his proposal to make me an artistic drawing
gratuitously. I almost feared I was being made
fun of, and looked most significantly at my
friend Tarquinio. He understood me, and exclaimed:

— Bartolo, this gentleman is the Cavalier
Antonio Cua, an illustrious professor of mathematics in the Royal University of Naples; he
is one of the best men in the world. He offers
to lend you his gratuitous services; rest assured you will have a satisfactory plan.

This to me was like a revelation, and slightly bowing my head, I whispered: — Providence has led me to meet an engineer who is
the senior Professor of the University. — For
It seemed to me that Heaven had lent me a
visible sign of its protection. I felt quite overcome. Here indeed — thought I — is a thread
God has placed in my hand, without even my
seeking it.

While thus thinking, I uttered a few words of thanks. I felt however, quickly impelled to speak of the merit there must be in God's Sight, for any one who builds a temple to the Lord; and cited the wonders performed in a short time by the Virgin of Pompei, in favour of those who had helped towards this work of charity and salvation.

Professor Cua, whose heart was as noble as his mind, exclaimed :

— Well! as you are building a church for poor peasants, and with pennies not easily collected, I not only will give you the design, but I shall myself, and without any remuneration whatso ever, superintend the work of the building at Pompei: when I go to and fro, the cost of travelling will be mine.

. .

Beside myself with joy, I immediately wrote as follows to Valle:

Dear Don Gennaro,

Suspend all work! The Lord has stretched forth His hand to help me. He has brought me in contact with an engineer a learned Profes-

sor at the University, who has offered to direct
the building of the church without fee or compensation; and what is more generous still,
he does not even wish to have his travelling
expenses refunded.

It is therefore plain that the Lord assists
us visibly. Let us take courage. I shall come
to Valle next week, in the meantime our undertaking is to be announced from the pulpits
of some of the churches in Naples where larger
congregations assemble. Fare you well.

Naples, May 20th 1876.

YOUR BARTOLO LONGO.

Thus at last a substantial beginning was
given to the building of the temple, which was
within so short a time to rise a very marvel
of beauty and splendour.

CHAPTER II.

June 8ᵗʰ 1876.
The first apparition of the Virgin of Pompei.
Madam Giovannina Muti.

Meanwhile I left no stone unturned, still
further to spread information regarding the
work that had been undertaken in Pompei,
among the Neapolitan people.

But Providence Itself, as ever, was my best
coadjutor.

It was the first of June of that same year
1876. The Countess and I were visiting many
different Neapolitan families, to collect the
monthly penny subscriptions in order to continue the building of the foundations.

Of all our friends and acquaintances, we
asked the names and addresses of good and
generous persons, who would be willing to
subscribe a penny a month.

Among others, we were told to apply to
a wealthy and charitable family, Laghezza
by name, residing in Via Sᵗᵃ Teresa, N. 75.

Thither we bent our footsteps. This was on the 6th of June.

But kindly as the ladies received us, on hearing our request, they seemed unable to credit our statements, and to prevent further importunity, exclaimed: — It is impossible to build a church on penny subscriptions — as much as to say — abandon such utopian ideas.

Then in order to win them over to our side, we began telling them of the various wonders performed by the Virgin of the Rosary, in favour of those who helped in the work with these simple penny subscriptions.

— Oh, if Our Lady would but vouchsafe to perform a wonder! — exclaimed Madame Caroline, mother of the family, — to-day would be the time to manifest her power. Our good friend, Madame Giovannina Muti, has left our house in the most critical state of health to go to Villa Doria, on the Vomero. And the owner of the house, knowing that she must die of consumption there, has inserted in the contract that payment must be obligatory for three years; upon the decease of the lady, the whole apartment will have to be renovated at the expense of the family. Her physician has to-day told us that there is no hope for her.

All her friends, and we among them, are oppressed with sorrow. Her affectionate husband,
Sig. Ferdinand Muti, is inconsolable. She will
leave behind her five orphanl children.

— If this be so — we answered — tell your
friend to have recourse to the Virgin of the
Rosary, Who for the building of her church
in Pompei to-day grants most singular favors.

— If you only knew — interrupted one of the
ladies — how many vows her husband has
made, how many gifts he has presented to
various churches and all in vain. He has now
lost all hope.

— We ask no vows or gifts — we answered.—
Induce your friend to try what others have
tried so efficaciously. Here is a sheet of paper
for Promoters.

So saying I drew forth and placed beneath
the ladies' eyes a sheet of printed paper bearing this simple heading: *For a Temple in
Pompei.* Let the patient inscribe her name at
the head of the page with the small offering
of a *sou a month* for the new Temple of Mary
and seek to find other subscribers. In other
words let her begin to act as Promoter of Our
Lady, who never fails to recompense all who
labor for Her and at the same time promise

to publish the miracle should it be granted
her.

That same evening the Misses Laghezza
sent a letter to their dying friend, beseeching
her to vow herself to the miraculous Virgin
of the Rosary of Pompei, and making her promise to inscribe herself as Promoter of the
new church there to be erected.

.˙.

Madam Giovannina Muti, nee Sabbato, lay
indeed at death's door. Such indeed was the
state of her health that not only had her doctors given up every vestige of hope but many
had already thought her to be deceased.

It was in this sad condition of things that
the poor lady received the letter written her
by the Misses Laghezza. On reading the lines
of her friends and the programm of the church
of Pompei inclosed in the letter, her heart
was deeply touched, and she immediately
wrote her name on the subscription sheet,
and then called her mother, her maid, and
so on all her family.

And such was the sudden faith she felt in
her heart scarce had she written her name

that from that very moment she felt sure of the desired miracle.

. .

It was the eighth day of June. But a month had elapsed since Our Lady had with a smile of blessing looked down upon the humble valley of Pompei, where a work had been begun *that heaven and earth alike were to lay their hand to.*

Madam Muti fell into a slumber, during which she seemed to behold the Virgin of the Rosary seated on a throne, with her Infant on her arms and the rosary in her hands, but without a diadem on her brow. It was thus indeed that the Virgin was depicted in the old painting venerated in Pompei; but of this fact the invalid knew nothing as she had never beheld the picture.

It seemed to her that the Virgin gazed most tenderly upon her, while she besought her with tears and groans to free her from her sufferings and to obtain her recovery from her divine Son. And while weeping she pointed, being unable to speak, to the Babe, as though imploring her health through the in-

tercession of the Virgin. When lo and behold
the merciful Mother Mary smile and look at
her steadily, and throw a white ribbon to her
on which were written some words, which
she hastened to read: *The Virgin of the Ro-*
sary of Pompei has granted her request to the
invalid Giovannina Muti.

— Oh Mother of the Rosary! Oh Mother, I
hope so! Sayest thou true?... Shall I indeed
be spared? Will I not die?... thus she spoke
in her vision.

The vision vanished; she scarce could believe herself; it all appeared to her a dream.
But it had not been a dream, for she had heard
the words and movements of the people who
were in the adjoining room. Was it then really
an apparition of the Virgin of the Rosary? But
how was she to explain the fact of the Virgin
of the Rosary being seated and without a
diadem on her brow, where as she is always
depicted everywhere standing, in a queenly
attitude, and with the royal diadem on her
brow? What meant then this unusual attitude?

The poor invalid could find no answer to
these questions. Yet nevertheless she felt as
though new life throbbed in her veins. She
felt elated as though with a sudden and in-

tense joy. Her emotion did not allow her to
relate what had occurred, and yet how hide
it? Why not rejoice the hearts of her dear
ones with the rays of a hope they no longer
felt?

Taking courage she called to all to surround
her and then related her vision.

Instantly all fever and the obstinate cough
disappeared.

While the fortunate woman was still relating
with growing warmth and vividness what had
happened, her husband, Sig. Ferdinando Muti
returned home.

As soon as the latter beheld his wife, whom
he already wept as dead, seated in bed and
conversing with a voice never interrupted by
that suffocating cough, and telling of the
strange occurrence, overcome by emotion he
flew downstairs to the stables, mounted a
horse and dashed off toward Naples to learn
all the facts of the case from the ladies Laghezza.

On entering their room he fell on his knees
before Madam Carolina and moved to tears
thus spoke:

« You have restored unto me my wife! » and
forthwith he told them of the vision and of

the sudden improvement, asking at the same time the meaning of the words *Virgin of Pompei.*

The pious Misses Laghezza quite overcome with surprise could offer him no other explanation than the *visit of two strangers who had come to solicit subscriptions of a sou a month for a church to be built in Pompei and to be dedicated to the Virgin of the Rosary.* Nothing else did they add, nor say that the Virgin in the Image was not crowned, and the like.

But there the fact was! Madam Muti had seen the Virgin as she was depicted in Pompei, and from a dying condition had instantaneously returned to new life.

Full of holy joy the Misses Laghezza, feeling that the Madonna had made use of them to accomplish a miracle, hastened to give notice of what had happened to Rev. Father Altavilla, whom they had heard a few days before pronounce from the pulpit of the church of S. Domenico Soriano words of enthusiasm concerning *a catholic church in Pompei to be erected with monthly subscriptions of a sou.*

Father Altavilla rejoiced at hearing such glad news hastened to inform the Countess and myself. Thus all three of us on June 31th betook ourselves to the villa Doria on the Vomero to hear the marvellous tale from the lips of the invalid. And Madam Muti most frankly, like a person in perfect health, repeated the facts to us.

On August 30th the fortunate lady returned to Naples, completely cured and free from all ailments, arousing universal wonder in all who knew her.

With her own hand she wrote the history of the case and Father Altavilla read the same to a numerous congregation in the church of St. Nicholas of Tolentino.

Madam Muti's mother offered fifty francs toward the building of the Temple. Her son, Pietro Muti, a priest's cape. A silver lamp and pyx, inscribed with the name of Giovannina Muti, are kept in the Sanctuary as a perpetual memory of the first apparition of Our Lady of the Rosary under her new title of *Virgin of Pompei,* apparition that took place on the 8th day of June 1876, a month after the laying of the cornerstone of the Temple of Mary.

Madam Muti is still living to-day, nineteen years after that date, and all who visit her and knew how she was on the brink of the grave, cannot refrain from marveling and praising God.

And nothing rejoices her more than to relate the miracle received and attribute it to the *most miraculous Virgin of the Rosary of Pompei.*

CHAPTER III.

An offering for the first Altar.
Madam Rachel De Hippolytis.

It was evident then that Heaven wished to encourage and strengthen us and to teach us to stand firm whatever seeming adversities and contrarieties might arise.

And behold, before the expiration of that same month of June, Mary granted still other favors and graces.

Among the pious listeners to Father Altavilla in the church of San Domenico Soriano on the morning of May 24th, was a certain gentlewoman, Rachele De Hippolytis by name, who resided in Via S. Spirito di Palazzo N. 41. Her son lay gravely ill with a complication of diseases. On hearing from the lips of the fervent orator that the Virgin lavished daily favors upon all who took an interest in the new church of Pompei, she felt new hope kindle within her, and said to herself:

—Oh! if the Virgin of the Rosary of Pompei would but give me back my son!.... I would offer a *thousand* francs with which to build the *first altar* in that church.

And the Queen of Mercies poured her heavenly balsam on the sore heart of the afflicted mother. Madam De Hippolytis had not yet returned home and her son was already out of danger and in a short time he was restored to perfect health.

But the love of a mother, when the health of her children is in question, is always dubious and inclined to fear the worst.

Thus Madam De Hippolytis cannot believe her own eyes; she is in constant dread of a bitter disillusion. She wants to ascertain whether the recovery of her son will be able to brave and withstand the rigors of the following winter. And so she allowed the year 1876 and all the winter of 1877 to roll by. But when the next May returned and still found her son enjoying perfect health, she felt the sting of remorse for not having sooner kept her pro-

mise to Our Lady, and decided in her heart
to repair her failing generously.

— *I will not only give a thousand francs* —
thus spoke she to herself, — *but the interest
on the same for a year, one hundred and fifty
francs, beside.*

And so as to render still more signal witness
to the favor received she went personally to
Nola and placed the sum of one *thousand one
hundred and fifty francs* in the hands of the
venerable Bishop with the request that he
send them to the founders of the Temple for
*the first altar to be built in the church of the
Rosary of Pompei.*

CHAPTER IV.

The foundations strengthened.

Towards the first days of July the illustrious
Professor Antonio Cua betook himself for the
first time to Pompei, carrying with him the
architectural drawing of the new church,
which he had been obliged to accomodate to
the dimensions fixed by me with the excavation
of the first foundations.

First of all he showed us the great error of building an edifice, especially the foundations, by piecemeal.

— If you next year should lay new foundations and on them construct a new portion of building you will find that in joining the new construction to the old they will seperate; for the part first built will naturally settle before the newly built part, which when it in its turn comes to settle will naturally draw away from the older portion and thus inevitably produce a damage.

It was therefore necessary to open all the foundations at once, and as they were to bear an enormous weight, for the stones to be used in the building were volcanic, it was but prudent to construct them of solid masonry. Those already built were solidified so as to render them perfectly secure.

But for the execution of his design he needed a more able mason. Hence Pasquale Vitiello, the master mason of Scafati, who had measured the church of Our Lady of the Muroli with me, was recalled.

Work on the church was resumed under the direction of engineer Cavalier Cua on the 10th of August of that year, and up to that date

thousand two hundred francs had been spent,
beside the gratuitous gifts of stones, mortar
and labor.

CHAPTER V.

The first feast within the enclosure of the foundations.

Six months had not yet elapsed from the
day of the laying of the cornerstone of the
new Temple and already the foundations of
the House of the Lord had been laid.

Toward the middle of October the superfi-
cies of the great underground masonwork had
already reached the level on which the holy
habitation was to rise, and the whitewashed
surface formed a pleasing contract to the dark
earth lying round about.

The reader will remember that for four years
past I had never allowed the month of October
to go by without festing the Queen of the Rosary with the peasant folk of the valley; therefore it was more than ever right and just
to celebrate her festivity now and within that
rough enclosure. The feast was to consist prin-

cipally in offering to God the *first Sacrifice*
on that land bought for the manifestation of
His glory.

Two barrels were placed at the further extremity, and across them were laid planks
covered with linen and drapery. Thus an altar
similar to the one erected on the 8th day of
May was improvised. On it were placed a
Crucifix, six candles and a sacred stone. Above
the altar, against a background of white and
blue draperies was hung the old Image, not
yet retouched by Maldarelli, and hence not
very pleasing to the sight, but dear indeed
to me as a signal of victory, and by many
venerated as a source of divine consolations.

The feast was ordered for the last Sunday
of the month which fell on the 29th.

Fair indeed was that morning on which the
Queen of the Most Holy Rosary was fêted for
the first time by her children on the spot
chosen by Herself as her new dwelling-place,
as a throne of her mercies.

On the area of the growing Sanctuary, on
that land where in days of yore the demon
had been adored, beneath a humble tent the
bloodless Sacrifice of expiation and of love
to the true and living God was for the first

time offered up. Round about in the open country, scattered over with volcanic stones, stood a motley crowd of nobles and plebeians, who had come from Naples and the out lying towns, and who in the presence of the venerable Bishop of Nola devoutly recited the fifteen decades of the Holy Rosary of Mary.

The sacred orator whom I invited to preach during that strange yet poetical service, celebrated by the side of a provincial highway, was the same Father Altavilla who had by his sermons aroused such a flame of devotion in Naples toward the Virgin of Pompei.

With most tender words of love and faith the eloquent orator recalled the perennial triumph of the cross over barbarism, over heresy and paganism; and as constant companion of every new victory Mary, sweet Mother of mankind. He observed how She had not chosen a great and populous city in which to be duly honored but had wished to plant her seat in a barren country, on gentile land, among the toiling children of the soil.

Oh all who were present in that hour did indeed taste of the ineffable joys that true religion imparts to the soul.

Opposite rose Mount Vesuvius with its to-

wering crest of smoke; to the left the amphitheatre with its ruins of pagan civilization,
and behind the same all the broken remains
of a dead city still bearing the imprint of its
gentile customs; beneath our eyes an enclosure of masonwork still damp with the early
autumn rains; and there beneath our gaze a
Crucifix that has the power to rennovate and
restore all things, and above It another image,
dear, sweet image, the image of the Mother
of the Crucified, and Mother of the redeemed
as well.

Precious tears coursed down the cheeks of
the listeners. Those tears were the words of
the believer's heart speaking to God in a voice
of mingled love and sorrow. It was the voice
of sorrow at the sight of so many modern
impieties and heresies; it was the voice of
love and gratitude to God, Who deigns to accept for His glory the works of man, and o-
penly marks His acceptance of them by means
of the miracles granted at the invocation of
the *Virgin of the Rosary of Pompei.*

Such was the impulse of love and faith a-
roused in that hour in the hearts of all that
the holy Bishop of Nola himself, unable to
master his emotion, descended from his seat,

and placing himself in the midst of the people, with burning words exhorted them to the catholic faith, and intoned the Apostles Creed in which all present joined him. Oh our Religion in the grandeur of its truth is indeed surrounded with enchanting beauty.

CHAPTER VI.

The year 1876.

That feast marked the close of the first year of the origin of the Sanctuary, as it was against the interest of economy to build during the winter when the days are short and rain and storms frequent, all the more so as I paid the workmen by the day. Beside which the Countess and I spent the winter months in the effort to procure new Associates.

I find in my primitive registers that up to the fifteenth of November I had spent *seven-thousand three hundred and seventy francs* and *ten* centimes.

Now the amount of the offerings collected was *four thousand nine hundred and forty five francs* and *eighty five* centimes. Hence there

was a deficit of two thousand fourhundred
and thirty four francs and thirty five centimes,
to pay for stones, mortar and so forth.

On the day of the feast I exposed a tablet
bearing the names of all contributors and the
amount of their contribution, beside the sums
total of both *income* and *outlay*, signed by
Engineer Chevalier Antonio Cua.

At sight of the great difference betwen my
income and my outlay the good Bishop of
Nola was greatly taken aback and remon-
strated with me, recalling his precept never
to spend more than one has in hand.

But as far back as that time I felt within
me a strength and vigor which certainly were
not natural, for while my body was weak and
feeble because of severe infirmities sustained,
my spirit was dominated by a holy enthusiasm which allowed me but to think of the
Temple of the Lord in Pompei.

I beheld it rise pure and holy in my mind's
eye, and the profound conviction laid hold on
me that it was God's will a church should
rise on that spot, and that hence, were men
willing or not, nothing could impede His designs. And so I quickly tranquilized the prudent Prelate, by assuring him that I gladly

took that debt and all other debts to come upon my own shoulders, sure that Heaven would not have forsaken me.

From that day to this I have unflinchingly followed that line of conduct; results prove that I was right.

Certainly I was acting most contrary to the dictates of human prudence, but I reasoned thus, not according to worldly philosophy but according to that of the Saints.

When from the start God reveals Himself in an undertaking by an extraordinary intervention (and that by the voice of miracles), then through His infinite goodness and ineffable mercy, the man whom He places at the head of this work, becomes an instrument of His Providence, and He inspires him together with a great desire of good with a certainty of success. Neither does He allow him to be frightened by obstacles, but invigorates him with the vision of the final outcome.

Thus it was that through mere divine mercy I took no heed in those days of mens' judgments of me and of my undertaking, which naturally, according to mere appearances, seemed strange to say the least, or the result of religious enthusiasm.

The events of that memorable year alone influenced me and from that moment, realizing that I was but an instrument in the carrying out of a divine design, I fixed my eyes unflinchingly on Him, Whose work I felt it to be, and trod the path laid out for me, hoping all things from above.

In the second Volume of the History of this Sanctuary the reader will easily gather how well founded was my faith, and on beholding the works of the Lord will realize how small and insignificant are man and his plans. Then truly will his heart exult and he will exclaim with the Psalmist:

" Come and behold ye the works which the Lord has wrought „.

CONTENTS

BOOK SECOND

The New Valle di Pompei.

BOOK THIRD

The Miraculous Image.

BOOK FOURTH

The foundations of the Temple.

www.ingramcontent.com/pod-product-compliance
Lightning Source LLC
Chambersburg PA
CBHW020849020726
47497CB00005B/1319